You are about to set off on an adventure in which you will meet many dangers—and face many decisions. Your choices will determine how the story turns out. So be careful . . . you must choose wisely!

DO NOT READ THIS BOOK FROM BEGINNING TO END!

Instead, as you are faced with a decision, follow the instructions and keep turning to the pages where your choices lead you, until you come to an end. At any point, your choice could bring success—or disaster!

You can read *Claw of the Dragon* many times, with many different results. So if you make an unwise choice, go back to the beginning and start again!

GOOD LUCK ON YOUR ADVENTURE!

Endless Quest ™

CLAW of the DRAGON

Bruce Algozin

MIRRORSTONE

Claw of the Dragon

©1986, 2008 Wizards of the Coast, Inc.

Published by Wizards of the Coast, Inc. ENDLESS QUEST, MIRRORSTONE, and their respective logos are trademarks of Wizards of the Coast, Inc., in the U.S.A. and other countries.

Printed in the U.S.A.

Cover art by Tim Jessell
First Printing: September 1986
This Edition First Printing: January 2008

Cataloguing in Publication data is available from the Library of Congress

9 8 7 6 5 4 3 2 1

ISBN: 978-0-7869-4719-5
620-21523740-001-EN

U.S., CANADA,
ASIA, PACIFIC, & LATIN AMERICA
Wizards of the Coast, Inc.
P.O. Box 707
Renton, WA 98057-0707
+1-800-324-6496

EUROPEAN HEADQUARTERS
Hasbro UK Ltd
Caswell Way
Newport, Gwent NP9 0YH
GREAT BRITAIN
Save this address for your records.

Visit our web site at www.mirrorstone.com

In this book you are Tory, a young settler on your kingdom's frontier. Life is difficult in the farming village, especially since your father became ill. And it has become even more difficult since the dragons began raiding your land.

The past several weeks, dragons have burned barns, fields, and even houses. The villagers have organized groups to keep watch during the night. They man huge wooden catapults, hoping to keep the dragons at bay; but the monsters have become more vicious, and the catapult stones no longer deter them. Some villagers are worried about what will happen if the dragons ever come all at once. No one seems to know what's behind the raids, and so they can't do anything to stop them.

You would never admit this to anyone, but you actually look forward to the attacks, for they may be your family's salvation. The stones from the catapults loosen scales from the dragons' massive bodies, and the dragons' scales are extremely valuable. Your family needs whatever gold you can earn to keep *yourselves alive until the crops on your small farm can be harvested . . . if they can ever be harvested, what with the repeated dragon raids. You and Barnaby spend almost every day hunting for the fallen scales. You've been scale-hunting for most of the morning, when you discover something that will change your life . . . .*

"There's nothing here," your brother Barnaby says, poking among the rocks with a stick. "We might as well go home. We're not going to find any more dragon scales today."

"Don't give up so easily," you say. "Let's go on just a bit farther." You walk up a curving path that leads onto a narrow ridge. You've only found two dragon scales this morning, and one of them was cracked. You've got a good feeling about the valley on the other side of the ridge, though. Just past a stand of pine trees, you know the path descends to a wide valley that the dragons always fly across as they flee your catapults.

Barnaby scrambles after you. "But it's hot, and I'm getting sunbur—"

A terrifying shriek breaks off Barnaby's complaint. The cry reverberates off the walls of the valley below until it sounds like a dozen howling beasts. Barnaby grips your arm.

"What was that?" you say. "Come on! Let's see." You run up the rough rocks until you reach the pine trees on the edge of the ridge, with Barnaby following behind. Together, you and Barnaby part the stiff branches and look out on a stony depression.

Below you, not fifty feet away, two dragons—a red and a gold—are fighting.

Piercing screams tear the air as the dragons thrash and claw and try to burn each other with their flaming breath. It looks as if the red one is winning.

Glittering scales litter the ground beneath the fighting dragons. Your heartbeat quickens. If you can manage to gather them all, your family will live well for the rest of your life.

The red backs the gold against a large rock and hooks the gold's shoulders with its monstrous foreclaws. With the long talons on its hind feet, the red rips into the gold's underside. The gold screams in pain, its cries echoing against the rocks and filling the canyon.

"It won't be long before the red one finishes the gold off," Barnaby says. "Then we can grab the scales."

"Shhh!" you whisper.

The gold dragon surprises you both. With a beat of its wings, it throws off its adversary, and suddenly the two are on an equal footing again, circling each other, looking for openings as though they've just begun to fight. But despite the gold's heroic effort, it's still bleeding and very much the worse for wear.

The red dragon senses this. In a flash, it leaps on its foe again with an incredible surge of energy. The gold goes down and hardly puts up a fight as the red's claws and teeth dig into its back and tear at its flesh.

Several minutes pass before the red backs off. The gold doesn't move.

For a brief moment, the red stands over its victim, its back to you. It pecks at the gold and picks at its foe's body with its claws. The red marches several paces on its strong legs, spreads its wings, and takes flight.

"Come on!" Barnaby begins to push his way through the tree limbs. "Now's our chance."

You pull your scaling knife from the scabbard on your belt and follow Barnaby toward the fallen dragon. You've never stripped a whole dragon before. It could take weeks. You might as well get started.

Then you notice a slight throb in one of the dragon's leathery wings. You catch Barnaby by the arm.

"It's not over yet," you say. "Wait until the gold's dead."

Sure enough, no sooner do you say this than the great dragon attempts to stand. A lonely wail issues from its torn throat. "Clyto!" it shouts. "Come back! You'll pay for this, Clyto, you villain!"

You and Barnaby stare at the dragon. You may have had plenty of experience with dragon attacks and scales, but you've never heard one talk!

"Clyto!" the dragon wails once more.

For all his bravery, the gold is faltering. It stumbles to the ground, beating its wings furiously and struggling to raise its head.

Barnaby takes the knife from your hand and pushes past you toward the dragon. You stop him again.

"Where do you think you're going?" you say.

"To put an end to it."

"Why? It won't live much longer."

"It's ruining its scales, that's why. If it keeps tossing itself around like that, it's going to look like someone took a hammer to them. I'm just going to put it out of its misery."

"But . . . but it talks!"

"I know it talks. But so what? Its scales won't be worth any more because of it."

"Yes, but if it can talk, maybe it can tell us why the dragons have been attacking the village."

"The dragons attack because they're mean and they hate us. Now stand back, Tory. I've got to do this while it's lying still."

Should you let Barnaby kill the dragon? Or should you talk to the huge creature and try to solve the mystery of the dragons and their dislike for the villagers?

If you decide to let Barnaby kill the dragon, turn to page 25.

If you want to try to talk to the dragon, turn to page 42.

You lean over the ledge. Barnaby's still at the end of the rope. By some miracle the rope tangled around his arm. Even though one of the falling rocks seems to have knocked him out, he's still alive, dangling some eighty feet below.

"Psst! Tory!" Finn beckons to you from behind the rock.

All you can think about is Barnaby. You can't leave him like this! There's no time to check the attachment holding the end of the rope, or even to see if the rope will hold your additional weight. Terrified, you lower yourself over the ledge.

The rope stretches to its limit, but it holds. Below you, the river flashes without letup. Now and then you pause to look down at Barnaby. He looks pale in the river's eerie glow.

It's probably good he was knocked out, you think. If he were thrashing around down there, it might be enough to snap the rope.

"Tory!" Finn calls from above, but you ignore him, your mind set on one thing only.

You're getting closer. The time has come to think how you're going to rescue Barnaby. You're going to have to wake him somehow, and you hope he has enough strength to cling to your back. You won't be able to hold on to him and climb too.

"Tory!" Finn shouts.

You're almost there. You look down and see your brother starting to come to. Just don't panic when you wake up and see where you are, Barnaby! you think.

"Tory!"

You glance up, irritated, wondering what in the world the little leprechaun could want. Nothing in all your experience could have prepared you for what you see.

Standing on the rock ledge above you is the largest person you've ever seen. Her head must be a full four feet wide! You can't even begin to estimate the girth of her broad waist or the length of her incredibly long legs, but she seems to fill the entire cavern.

She's looking down at you in fascination, her green eyes glittering in the flashes from the river. To your horror, you see her reach for the rope.

You feel the fragile strand jerked powerfully upward, and you and Barnaby fly straight up, away from the river. Suddenly, the rope snaps somewhere near the top and you're falling into the swirling, flashing waters below.

The water hurls you along more swiftly than the fastest horse. There's no chance of swimming or trying to fight the current. You can only struggle to keep your head above water as you're tumbled and thrown about in the wild water, out of the cavern, and into a dark watercourse where the only light is the river flashing.

You've lost sight of Barnaby—not that there was any hope of keeping track of him. You can only pray that he's all right.

The river carries you for a long time, battering and hammering you with an anger that never seems to end. Then finally, almost without you realizing it, the river spills into a vast underground lake, and in a few minutes you find yourself staggering onto a beach. To your amazement, Barnaby is waiting for you.

"Tory!" he exclaims when he sees you. "You'll never guess what I found!"

"Are you all right?" you ask him.

"Yeah, just wet. Listen to me! Guess where we are? Can you feel the heat?"

"Yes . . ." you say, still trying to catch your breath. "It's hot. So what?"

"Dragons, Tory!" Barnaby says. "Dragons search out mountains that are hot like this."

"You mean—"

"Yes! We're in the Ayrie! We made it!"

You look around. On the domed ceiling over the lake, lights flicker as though somewhere ahead of you a fire is burning.

"There's a tunnel over there," Barnaby says, pointing towards the flickering.

"Good," you say. "Let's go find some dragons."

Please turn to page 171.

The opening to the tunnels is a small square hole in the side of the mountain, supported by half-rotted timbers. Oskar leads the way, and the rest of you follow.

Inside, it's dank and musty. Your footsteps echo eerily on the tunnel floor, and after the first hundred feet, the opening is no longer visible behind you. The four of you are alone in the dark tunnel, with only Oskar's weak torch to see by.

The air smells of damp earth, and you find it difficult to breathe. The walls seem as though they're closing around you, and you think of all the stories you've heard of miners trapped in cave-ins.

"What's the chance of a cave-in?" you ask Oskar.

The old dwarf pauses, as if he's listening to the earth around you. "Hmm. Pretty good, I'd say."

You shift your pack uneasily on your back. The claw feels as heavy as a brick. You wonder if you'll ever get it delivered.

Hours pass by. Every now and then, Oskar calls for a rest. You plop down and try to catch your breath, but no matter how hard you try, it doesn't seem to do any good. It's as though the air has already been used.

Oskar and Finn don't seem to be affected. They've taken to arguing between themselves, and they go at it with remarkable energy.

The procession comes to an abrupt halt. You see at once what the problem is. The tunnel has split into two identical trails leading off in opposite directions, one to the left and one to the right. Oskar stands in the intersection and scratches his head.

"This one," he says, pointing to the left-hand tunnel. "No . . . Maybe this one." He gestures to the right. "I . . . I can't seem to remember."

"It's the right-hand path you want," says Finn firmly. "A leprechaun's instinct is never wrong."

"No, I'm sure it's to the left," says Oskar.

"To the right, I say!" says Finn.

They'll be at each other's throats in a minute. You're going to have to settle the argument, but which path is it? Do you listen to the leprechaun, who has been fairly lucky . . . even though he couldn't find the way to the Storm Giant? Or do you believe the old dwarf, who seems to know the tunnels . . . but whose memory seems to be fading?

18

If you want to take Oskar's advice and go to the left, turn to page 21.

If you decide to trust Finn's instinct and take the other tunnel, turn to page 185.

I've thought about it. We've got to let Finn try his spell," you say, pulling away from your brother.

"But what if it doesn't work?" Barnaby catches your arm. "I don't know why I ever let you talk me into this crazy trip, Tory," he says. "We should have gone back and warned the village like I said in the first place."

"Aha!" Finn says, coming up suddenly and starting to dance around the two of you. "I've found the spell, I have!" He reaches up and takes each of you by the hand. "Come, come! The dragons await!"

He pulls you over next to the open book. "Stand just so."

He consults the book for a moment, then turns back to face the two of you and begins to mumble. The words mean nothing to you, but you know they are in the ancient language of magic. You don't pretend to understand them, but you notice that the landscape around you is beginning to change!

Slowly the rocks, and even the mountains themselves, become transparent. Even Finn's small figure, standing by the rock, is starting to dissolve.

"Finn!" you say. "Aren't you coming along?"

"No, my friend," he says. "It's not a spell you can cast and take part in too. I'm afraid my role in this adventure has come to an end."

"But, Finn! We still have to convince the dragons!" The little fellow has to come with you! What will you do without him?

"You're our good-luck charm, Finn," Barnaby says.

"Nay, nay. Your cause is just. That's better than luck."

"But, Finn . . ." you start to plead, but you can no longer see him. All around you, things are changing. Lights swirl. The air feels heavy. Objects appear out of the haze. You can make out torches set in brackets high on a rock wall. The torches are in the shape of dragons!

This must be the Ayrie, you think.

Please turn to page 171.

You decide to take Oskar's advice and follow the left-hand tunnel.

This tunnel is dustier than the others. The dust gets in your eyes and nose and makes it even more difficult to breathe. You grow ever more anxious to get out of these underground passages.

Oskar calls for a rest near a passage leading up out of the tunnel. You can feel a draft of fresh air from the shaft, so you decide to climb it to see where it leads.

You soon discover a ladder in the shaft, which makes your ascent easier. As you climb, the air becomes steadily cooler and more breathable.

When you reach the opening of the shaft, you poke your head out and look around cautiously. You're outside. The night is clear, and the stars shine brightly. The dark shapes of the mountains, cut like black silhouettes from the night sky, are unfamiliar to you.

You're in some sort of depression, with mountains on all sides of you. You pull yourself out of the opening and take a deep breath. The air is fresh and cool, much better than in the tunnel, but it carries a peculiar smell. It's hard to say what it is exactly—something animal, but nothing like your horses or cows.

You're wondering about it when you see something in the moonlight that stops you short. It's a round object, pure white and almost as tall as you are. Except for its size, it looks like a chicken egg.

You walk over to it and rap on its side. "If this is an egg," you wonder, "then how big is the bird that laid—"

You never finish the thought. A loud beating sound in the air above you fills your ears, and the wind picks up dramatically. You look up. Poised in the air is the largest bird you have ever seen! Its wings alone are as wide as the village's meeting hall!

You dash for the shaft opening, but you're too late. The creature has already seen you. With a screech so forceful it scatters the pebbles at your feet, it swoops down with its talons outstretched, ready to pick you up.

You dive for the opening and duck through

the narrow hole just in time. The monstrous bird's huge talons hit the ground beside the opening with a loud *THWACK!* The creature lets out a cry of frustration that seems to shake the entire mountain.

You scramble down the ladder as fast as your arms and legs can take you, your heart beating wildly in your chest.

When you have descended a safe distance, you stop to catch your breath. You can still hear the screeching and the savage beating of wings above you.

That's enough exploring, you think. Next time, I think I'll stick with the group.

You continue climbing down, eager to be reunited with your friends, when you notice something you didn't see before. The shaft splits into two identical tunnels reaching down into the blackness, one angling left, the other right. Both have ladders. You try to think, but for the life of you, you can't remember which way you came.

You pause on the ladder, feeling the terrible weight of indecision. Which one should you take—right or left? There's nothing to guide you.

You'll have to trust your gut.

24

If you want to take the shaft to your left, turn to page 153.

If you'd rather go to the right, turn to page 165.

You take a long look at the huge creature as it struggles with death. You love animals, and as a rule, you've always tried to protect them. But this one is an enemy. Its kind have burned the homes and crops of your neighbors in the village, homes that belonged to people you know. The dragon's fires have hurt friends and destroyed hours of labor.

Besides, you think, even if I talk to the dragon, there's no guarantee it would be friendly or tell the truth.

"All right, Barnaby," you say. "Go ahead and kill it."

Barnaby waits until the dragon quiets down, then leaps up onto its chest. The scales are slippery, but he manages to scramble up to a point right under the creature's jaw. It's here that a dragon's skin is thinnest and most vulnerable. The knife glistens as Barnaby raises it high.

At the last second, you look away, unable to watch. When you turn back, blood is gushing from a new wound in the dragon's neck.

What the red dragon left undone, your brother finishes in less than a second. The creature's huge body jerks violently, shaking Barnaby from his perch. Then the gold falls back and is still.

Barnaby catches his balance and hops onto a nearby rock. "That's better," he says wiping his hands off. "How much do you think Jasper will give us for all those scales?"

You stare up at the huge corpse, and you can't help but feel a twinge of regret. What secrets might the dragon have told you?

Barnaby holds the knife out in your direction. "We'd better get to it. This job's going to take the rest of the day."

By the time you've removed the prime scales, cleaned them, and tied them up in a bundle, the sun is a fiery ball on the western horizon. You check the bundle to make sure the scales are secure. Then the two of you start home.

The long walk seems even longer today. It must be because I'm so tired, you think. It's dark by the time you reach the village.

In your tiny cottage, your father is waiting in a chair by the fire.

"Where have you been?" he says as you come in. He starts to get up. He's been sick ever since you came into this mountain country, but tonight he looks even paler than usual.

"Hunting for dragon scales," you reply.

"And it was a good hunt too!" cries Barnaby, following you inside. He removes the pack from your shoulders, unlaces it, and spreads the gleaming dragon scales on the table. "We found a dragon, Father! A whole dragon! There were more scales. These were just the best. This should fatten that measly stipend we get from the king!"

"I should say so," your father says, stepping forward and looking at the treasure spread out on the crude wooden boards. He runs his hand over the scales' gleaming surfaces, his eyes glittering. "I should say so," he repeats. "Come, sit down, you two. Have some stew."

You spend dinner listening to Barnaby and your father talking about your newfound wealth and all the things you could do with it. You don't participate in the discussion. You're finding it harder and harder to get excited about the scales.

You had both agreed not to mention the talking dragon. It wouldn't do much good, you figured, and most people wouldn't believe you. But now unease settles over you, an ominous feeling that won't go away.

That night, you go to sleep in a thoughtful mood. For hours you lie in your loft bed next to your brother's, thinking.

The sky is beginning to pale as you finally drift off, and it seems you haven't been asleep more than a few minutes when you feel Barnaby's hand upon your shoulder, shaking you.

"Oh no, Tory! Wake up! Look!"

Barnaby has thrown open the loft door that looks out onto the yard and the mountains beyond. Your eyes strain to focus on what he's pointing at.

Then you see them, little more than specks against the red sky, but from their shape and the peculiar motion of their large wings, you can't mistake what you're seeing—dragons, hundreds of them, heading for the village!

"We've got to warn somebody!" Barnaby says, scrambling over the bed.

He disappears down the ladder, but you linger by the window, staring at the menace winging its way toward your village.

There are too many of them, you think. All the catapults in the kingdom can't stop them this time.

The gold dragon must have known this was coming. It's just a hunch, but you feel certain that it's true. If only you had stopped Barnaby from killing the dragon and tried to talk to it! You might have been able to prevent this! If only you had stopped to listen. . . .

I don't think either Barnaby or I want to be turned into ghosts, Finn," you say.

"You don't trust my magic, eh?" Finn says. "Well, I'll fight them alone, then. You'll see what Old Finn's made out of!"

With a look of determination, the little man hops off the rock. Then he turns his back to you and begins to mutter in a language that sounds more like a series of animal noises. Suddenly he disappears before your eyes!

"Where did he go?" asks Barnaby, wide-eyed. "Did he run away?"

"Shh!" you say. "Let's see what happens next."

In a moment, a new figure appears among the ghosts swarming before the wizard's door. Even though he's translucent, you can tell the figure is Finn. He looks just the same, but he's now three or four times his normal size.

With a mighty roar, Finn swoops down on the ghosts. Howling and screaming, they scatter like frightened sheep to the far corners of the chamber.

"Not bad," you say with a grin. Barnaby nods his approval.

But the ghosts are not yet defeated. They regroup quickly and charge Finn from all sides. When they hit him, the colors of your leprechaun companion's luminous figure begin to separate and turn murky and dull.

"I don't like the looks of this," you say.

"Me neither," Barnaby agrees. "Do you think the little guy's hurt?"

Before you can answer, Finn's ghostly shape disappears altogether. It's several seconds before it reappears, and when it does, Finn looks even more faded and dim. He's moving noticeably slower too.

"This is bad," you say. "We've got to do something!"

"What can we do?" Barnaby asks.

The ghosts swarm over Finn's weakened form like ants over a fallen lump of sugar. For a moment, Finn's shape is completely hidden from view. Then suddenly Finn bursts out from among the translucent shapes. He looks stronger now, and you can only guess he's called upon his last reserves of strength.

Finn charges the ghosts, amid a frightful

chorus of wails and sobs. Again and again he charges, until slowly, one by one, the ghostly figures begin to fade. At last the ghosts are gone completely.

When Finn returns to his solid form, you find him lying on the floor, his face pale. His little hand reaches out to you as you rush over to him.

"You shouldn't have done that, Finn!" you say. "You're hurt."

"Tory's right," says Barnaby, coming up behind you. "They might have killed you."

"Now, don't you two give me any guff," says the little fellow. "Go on, now. Go see your precious Old Man of the Mountain, although I don't think you'll find him to your liking."

"We can't just leave Finn here," says Barnaby.

"We'll have to take him with us," you say. "Between the two of us, we should be able to carry him."

"No!" says Finn emphatically. "I won't be dragged off to see that wizard! Not in this condition. He'll have me for sure, not being able to defend myself. Leave me be! Leave a torch behind, and when I'm all right again, I'll catch up."

You still can't bear the thought of leaving Finn behind, but if he won't be carried, your only alternative is to wait until he feels stronger. Waiting will only cost you precious time, and time is one thing you don't have to spare.

"What should I do?" you wonder.

If you decide to leave Finn behind, turn to page 39.

If you choose to wait until the little leprechaun feels stronger, turn to page 176.

W e'll follow the path with the lights," you say.

"Then I'm not going," the old dwarf replies.

"Are you sure?" asks Barnaby.

"I'm sure," the dwarf says. "You don't need a guide, and you don't listen to my advice anyway. Besides, being in this old mine just stirs up a lot of old memories."

"I'll be going back too," Finn says.

"You too?" you say. "I thought you were in this to the end. High adventure, you called it. Isn't that what leprechauns live for?"

"Aye, I've come with you this far, but you won't be needing me now. Now it's up to you to convince the dragons. That's political stuff. Magic and swashbuckling—that's more my line."

Barnaby is crushed. "But we need your help," he says. "You're our good luck charm."

"Well, thanks, my friend," Finn says. "But your cause is a just one, and when a cause is just, you've a fairer wind at your back than any leprechaun can provide."

"Are you certain you won't come?" you ask,

reaching down and taking the little leprechaun's hand.

"Aye, though I'll certainly miss you two," Finn says. "Now, the Ayrie's right through that passage. You can't miss it."

"How can you be so sure?"

"The heat," he says. "Don't you feel it? Dragons love it—seek it out, in fact. If it's possible to get to the Ayrie underground, that's got to be the way. But don't say a word to the old dwarf," he adds with a wink. "Let him think it was 'instinct.' "

"I'll miss you, Finn," you say sincerely.

"Of course you will," he says. "I'm difficult to replace. But enough of that, now. You've an urgent mission to perform. Better snap to it!"

You and Barnaby climb through the opening and start walking toward the lights. The last you see of Finn, he's following Oskar in the other direction, chattering excitedly about finding an adventure.

You discover Finn was right about the heat when you enter the new passage. It's oppressive. But it isn't long before you find yourself in a large hall with torches set in brackets high in the wall.

The brackets are carved in the shape of dragons, and you know you're in the Ayrie at last.

36   🗝 **Please turn to page 171.**

We appreciate your offer," you say to the old dwarf, "but I think we should go back the way we came. I still feel the Old Man of the Mountain is our best bet to get us to the Ayrie on time. That's where we were headed before Finn led us astray."

"As you wish," Oskar says, bowing graciously. "I wish you luck. I have no desire to see these skies filled with smoke from the fires of war."

"Astray, is it?" Finn says, once you're back on the trail. "How can you say I led you astray? It was you two who duped this poor old leprechaun into coming on this wild goose chase in the first place."

"You were excited to come," you remind him.

"And it was your idea to go see the Storm Giant, but you got us lost," Barnaby adds.

"Ach!" Finn says, screwing up his tiny face in disgust.

"Finn, we've got to reach the Ayrie," you say. "The lives of all our friends and their families depend on it. It isn't the time to be sulking."

"Now, don't be treating me like a child," Finn says. "I understand. I pledged to aid you, and aid you I shall. And you'll be needing it, too, or I don't know the Old Man of the Mountain."

"Then let's hurry. It'll be long past dark by the time we get there."

38

🔑 Please turn to page 108.

You rack your brain trying to make a decision. Finally, you say to Barnaby, "We'll have to leave Finn behind. We can't afford to take time to wait for him to recover."

"Now you're talking sense," the little man pipes up weakly. "You've your mission to think of. I'll be all right, I will."

"Are you sure this is the right decision, Tory?" asks Barnaby. "It seems pretty grim to leave him."

"It's a grim situation," you say. "The village itself is at stake. Here, give me your pack."

You stuff Barnaby's pack with a spare coat you brought along in case you got cold hunting scales. You gently ease it under Finn's head. You make sure he's as comfortable as you can make him, then say your goodbyes. You and Barnaby make your way to the Old Man's door and knock loudly.

The Old Man appears at the door, looking every bit as frightening and unfriendly as you imagined. He listens stone-faced to your story, then, without a word, motions you inside.

Something's wrong here, you think. This is too easy.

"I had a premonition you two might be visiting me," says the old sorcerer. "I thought you might bring magical protection, but I see you came alone."

He opens another door, and to your amazement, a gigantic figure looms in the doorway—Clyto, the same red dragon that killed Bosporus!

"Yes," Clyto says. "These are the two. I want them put to death."

"Let's not be needlessly harsh," the Old Man says. "Remember, I vowed to stay neutral in this matter. A simple spell will suffice." He waves his arms before him. . . .

Suddenly you start, as though awakening from a dream. You're home in the sleeping loft, next to Barnaby. The red dragon, the old wizard, even Finn and your quest to stop the dragon attack—all just a dream.

It's strange, but in a way, it's also a relief not to have to worry about saving the village. You jump from bed, feeling as though a great weight has been lifted from your shoulders.

You fling open the window. Dawn is just breaking, and the sun is a crown of gold on the horizon. Everything is going to be all right.

Suddenly, blotting the sun, you see shapes winging in your direction. Dragons! You go cold with realization.

It wasn't a dream after all! The dragons are really coming! All the Old Man had to do was cast a spell, and your quest came to an end.

You dash back to the beds. "Barnaby! Barnaby! Wake up! We have to warn the village!" you cry, but you know it's too late. . . .

Hold on, Barnaby. Let me talk to it. Just for a minute," you say. "Maybe I can find out something."

"Oh, all right," Barnaby says, tucking the scaling knife into his belt. "But hurry, will you? The scales will be worth more if they're in good shape."

You press past your brother and, hopping from stone to stone, cross the rocky terrain until you're just under the dragon's head.

The huge creature lies perfectly still, its eyelids shut tight. Its chest is still heaving, and blood flows from a wound in his throat, a thin trickle of crimson glistening on his magnificent scales.

"Um . . . Hello?" you say. You really have no idea how to address a dragon.

One huge eyelid springs open, and the dragon tries to lift its head to see you better. You want to run, but you stand your ground.

"We were nearby," you say. "We saw . . . what happened."

The dragon sighs, and its head falls back to the ground.

"Sir? Sir dragon? My brother and I—"

But before you can finish, a fit of violent coughing

seizes the dragon. When he stops, the dragon speaks again in a strained voice.

"Run back to your people. Warn them that they're all going to die."

"I don't understand. What are you talking about? Why are they going to die?"

The dragon gasps. "Tomorrow . . . at dawn. An attack on your village. Hundreds of dragons. They'll lay the town to waste."

"Just a minute," Barnaby says. You've been so busy listening to the dragon, you didn't hear him approach. "If you think we're going to give up without a fight, you're dead wrong. We've got our catapults ready, and we'll defend ourselves to end."

"Brave words!" the dragon says. "If you fight, you're sure to lose. There are too many of them. The village will be wiped out."

"But why?" you ask. "Why do the dragons attack us? We haven't done anything to them."

The dragon snorts. "You're settlers, aren't you? Paid by the king to farm the area?"

"There's nothing wrong with being paid to settle new land," Barnaby says. "It's done all the time. Why else would we come into a strange land just to scratch out a bare living? Besides, it helps the king extend his territory."

"Did you ever stop to think that all the land may not be free for the taking?" the dragon asks.

"Has someone staked a prior claim on the land we've settled?" you ask.

The dragon's head bobs up. "Prior claim!" he almost screams. "A dozen dragon clans lay claim to that land! Haven't you noticed the odd pockets of limestone embedded in the soil around here?"

Now that you think of it, there were a number of perfectly smooth, flat rocks just beneath the surface of the ground. It took a lot of effort to get them up when your father was plowing. You remember at the time wondering how they got there. They didn't look like any other rocks in the area.

"What are those rocks there for?" you ask.

"They're dragon nests," he says. "Once every century, when the mating season comes, we go to the plateau between the two mountains by the River Angol to hatch and rear our young."

"The River Angol? But that's right where our village is!" says Barnaby.

"So that's why you attack!" you say.

"Well, it doesn't matter," Barnaby says. "We've got farms there now, and our crops are planted. We're not going to move."

The dragon drops his head. "You don't understand," he says quietly. "I've just come from your king. We reached an agreement. He will move his settlement in return for . . . certain considerations."

"What considerations?" asks Barnaby.

"He's been promised the shells of the dragon eggs."

You remember hearing about the shells of dragons' eggs. They're said to be magic. Ground up and made into a broth, they are said to cure any disease. Some say they can even make an old man young.

Barnaby scowls. "No," he says, "the king wouldn't break his word. Not even for the shells of the dragon eggs. We're loyal subjects."

"The farmers will be paid five times what their land is worth," the dragon says. "The king made it a law."

"Five times its worth!" you cry, grabbing Barnaby's arm. "Did you hear that? We'll be rich!"

Barnaby pulls his arm away. "But we'd have to move," he says.

"So what?" you say. "We'll start over. We'll buy

a new farm somewhere near Tumin. The soil's better there, anyway."

"Maybe," says Barnaby, "but maybe this is just a trick."

"It's no trick!" the dragon says, then begins coughing again. When he finishes, his body trembles. You notice that a fine white powdery substance has begun to form on his nostrils.

"You must believe me," the dragon says. "What I tell you is the truth. I must get home! I must stop the others!"

There's no question in your mind that the dragon is dying. Tears begin to well in your eyes. "What . . . What if you can't get home?" you ask.

"I must stop the red dragon, or the others will surely attack the village!"

"The red dragon?" Barnaby says. "You mean the one you were fighting?"

"Yes!" the dragon says. "He's called Clyto. He wants to wear the mantle of leadership. He wants to be king of the dragons!"

"And he'll lead the attack?" you ask.

"Yes. He knew I was going to see your king. He waited for me here to ambush me. Now no one will know about the agreement until it's too late!"

"We have to do something," you say, turning to your brother. "We can't just let the dragon die like this!"

Barnaby shakes his head, then shrugs. The dragon coughs again, and makes long wheezing noises as it struggles to get its breath. The sound wrenches your heart.

"I'm afraid you're not going to make it, old fellow," you say softly. "I don't think you're ever going to see your home again."

"Then I've lost," the dragon says. "And so have you."

Your mind is filled with anguish. You feel something has to be done, and it's up to you and Barnaby to do it.

"What if my brother and I went to the other dragons for you and told them what's happened?" you say. "Would they believe us?"

"Tory!" Barnaby exclaims. Your words surprise even you.

"It's possible," says the dragon, "but you'll need a sign. Take the ring from my talon. It's King Olaf's ring. He gave it to me as a symbol of our new friendship."

You look at the dragon's front feet, which hang

limply on its chest.

"I don't see any ring," you say.

"Then that hateful Clyto has stolen it!" the dragon says. "We have no choice. You must cut off my claw. The claw will prove to the others that I sent you. A dragon would only give a claw to someone trustworthy."

You take your scaling knife from Barnaby and start toward the claw, but Barnaby grabs it back.

"What do you think you're doing?" he says. "You're not actually thinking of going to these dragons and trying to make peace, are you?"

"I don't have to. Peace has already been made. I just have to get them to believe it."

"But you can't . . . Wait a minute," he says, turning to the dragon. "Where is this place where we have to go to stop this attack?"

"The Ayrie," the dragon says, "at Dragon's Eye Peak."

"Dragon's Eye Peak?" Barnaby says. "Where's that?"

"The other side of the mountains," the dragon says.

"The other side of the mountains! And we have to be there by dawn By dawn tomorrow?"

"Yes," the dragon says. "Dawn."

"Well, that settles it, then, doesn't it?" Barnaby says. "We can't possibly make it by dawn. It's too far."

"Please! You must!" gasps the dragon. "Look for a friend, a dragon named Aurea. She knows the red dragon well. Tell her that Bosporus sent you. Show her the claw. She'll know you're telling the truth!"

The dragon begins coughing again. The terrible rasping sounds go on for almost a full minute. Finally they stop.

"I think it's dead," says Barnaby. He grabs hold of the great beast's shiny flank and begins to climb it, the scaling knife in his hand.

But the dragon is still alive. His huge snakelike head rears suddenly, throwing Barnaby back and into a scrubby bush.

"If all else fails, burn the claw!" the dragon gasps. Then his head falls back, and his great chest is still.

"What was that all about?" asks Barnaby, as you pull him out of the bush.

You shrug. You're finding it hard to speak. You only knew the creature for a short time, but there was something noble about the dragon. A lump is in your throat. You swallow hard, hoping Barnaby won't notice, but Barnaby notices everything.

"What's the matter with you, anyway?" he asks. "It's just a dragon."

"But he talked to us!" you shout, losing your temper. "He believed in peace! He gave his life trying to save us!"

"Right," says Barnaby. "But so what? He didn't succeed. The attack is still going to take place tomorrow, and in the meantime, these scales are going to rot out here in the sun."

"How can you think of scales at a time like this?" You take the knife from your brother, then push him aside and start climbing the dragon's chest toward the claw.

"You're going to go, aren't you?" Barnaby asks.

"I have to."

Barnaby sighs. "Then I guess I have to go too. I can't let you go alone."

Actually, you were hoping he'd say that. Your little brother can be a pain in the neck, but in a pinch he's a useful friend to have around. And it's going to be a long, hard journey across the mountains to the Ayrie.

"All right, then," you say. "We'll go together."

"Before we get carried away," Barnaby says, "let me point out one thing you may have overlooked. If we have any hope of reaching the other side of the mountains by dawn, we're going to have to leave now. That means there's no time to go back and warn the village about the attack. The village will be destroyed, and everyone in it will die if we can't stop the dragons. What are we going to do about that?"

You pause halfway up the dragon, struck by what your brother has said. Your heart sinks.

"He's right," you realize. "It's one or the other." Either you go back and warn the village, or you risk everything to make a headlong dash across the mountains and hope you reach the Ayrie in time. A horrible weight has been placed upon your shoulders. In the balance hangs the lives of hundreds of men, women, and children, all of them your friends. What should you do?

If you want to try to make it to the Ayrie by dawn, turn to page 66.

If you elect to return to warn the village, turn to page 119.

The ghosts drift back and forth, glowing eerily like sheets of light. You can't remember being more afraid, but if you want to save the village, you have to get past them.

"All right, Finn," you say, turning to the leprechaun, "how do we get by them?"

"You asked the right person, my friend. Ghosts are my specialty. More dangerous than a cave full of banshees they are too. Why, a ghost can age a child like you ten years, it can, just by laying its hand on you. Or it can kill you dead, depending on what pleases it. Only magic or silver can defeat them, but then it isn't defeating them we're worried about, is it? Merely skirting around them will suffice, and we might go about that in two ways.

"First, I could use a bit of my own magic and turn you and your brother here into something like ghosts yourselves. Then you could slip right by them, ghosts not being any too smart.

"Second, I could fight them. I'd win—at least

I always have in the past. But it lays me low, it does. Saps my strength. It's not easy fighting a ghost on its home ground, and I'm not getting any younger, like it or not."

Finn's words trouble you. Neither alternative he has suggested is to your liking. Yet the night is wearing on, and dawn is drawing ever nearer. You've got to decide on something. You draw Barnaby aside.

"What do you think?" you whisper. "Either we trust him to turn us into ghosts, or he fights the ghosts and maybe doesn't survive. Not much of a choice, is it?"

Your brother looks scared. "I don't like the idea of being turned into a ghost, Tory—not one bit. It makes me worry whether I'll ever get changed back to my normal self. Please don't make me!"

The same thought has occurred to you. You wonder whether it would be better to abandon this course of action altogether, and yet you remain convinced that the Old Man of the Mountain is your best bet to reach the Ayrie in time.

What should you do?

If you choose to let Finn
change you and your brother
into ghosts, turn to page 130.

If you decide to ask Finn to
fight the ghosts, turn to page
30.

You stoop down and run your fingers through the gold thoughtfully. It's a vast sum of money, easily enough to buy several new villages.

"All right," you say finally, "but someone will have to hurry back and warn the village of the attack."

"I'll go!" Barnaby says, hopping up.

"Fine," you say. "Then Finn and Oskar and I will stay here and guard the treasure."

"A capital idea!" Finn says.

You take Barnaby aside before he runs off.

"Don't tell the town anything about the dragon attack, only about all the gold," you say.

"Why?" Barnaby says.

"Because they'll all rush up here to see the gold," you say. "They won't know about the dragons until they get back and find the village gone. But if you tell them about the dragons, they'll want to stay and fight. People will get hurt. Just make sure everyone comes to see the gold."

Barnaby rushes off down the tunnel, leaving you with Oskar and Finn. The two old men seem to have settled their differences. They settle down to chat, while you take a seat atop the gold mound to think. You may not have saved your family and friends' homes, but you are saving their lives.

And what's more, you think, picking up a handful of the gold coins and watching them gleam in the torchlight, we'll be rich!

Psst, Barnaby! Let's choose the Eternal Fires, whatever they are."

Barnaby looks at you as though you've lost your mind. "Are you crazy?"

"If Clyto accuses us of being spies, no one will ever believe our story. He could say we killed Bosporus and took his claw. But if we choose the fires, we may still be able to escape."

Barnaby shakes his head. "You're asking me to sacrifice my life for the village. And we still might not be able to save the village!"

"Stop that whispering!" Clyto says. "What is your decision?"

"We choose the fires," you say.

Clyto grins evilly. "Very well! To the fires!"

Clyto summons guards who take away your scaling knife and bind your hands. Then they lead you down a long tunnel to the lowest level of the Ayrie. There they tie you on spits and suspend you over a fire in the floor. The fire seems to be made of molten rock and shimmers in the heat.

"This is the Eternal Fire of Dragon's Eye Peak," says Clyto, grinning broadly. "Of course, I *could* roast the two of you in a second with my fiery breath, but this will take much longer and be much more painful. Now, if you'll excuse me, I have urgent business with the council. I'll come check on you later."

Clyto leaves. The guards follow, and you and Barnaby find yourselves alone.

"Why in the world did you tell them you wanted to be roasted?" cries Barnaby.

The fire is beginning to sear your skin. Already you can feel blisters starting to form. To make matters worse, the guards left your pack on, and the claw is digging into your back.

"Shh!" you say. "Let me think! There's got to be some way out of this!"

Your bonds are made of leather. The more you struggle, the tighter they seem to become. There seems little chance of untying them. You realize you're going to have to come up with something else, and soon. The heat from the fire is growing unbearable.

"We need something sharp to cut the ropes," you say.

"Like what?" Barnaby replies. "They took our knife! All we have are our clothes, our shoes—"

"The claw!" you say.

You wriggle away from the spit so that your pack slides down your arms and hangs close to your fingers. By twisting and curling your fingers, you maneuver the dragon's sharp claw out of the bag and rub it against the leather until your bonds start to break.

It takes many long, sweltering minutes, and you nearly drop the claw, but soon you're free. You untie your brother.

"That was close!" says Barnaby, rubbing his wrists. "At least that claw's good for something."

You wish you could have used it to convince the dragons. "We've got to get out of here!" you say. "We need to find another way to stop the attacks."

You dismiss the idea of using the door. There could be guards. Then you notice an airshaft, which seems to lead to an even lower level. You decide to follow it.

The air in the shaft is stifling. Near the end you look out through a tiny opening into an underground cave, shimmering with molten lava.

"No wonder the Ayrie is so hot!" you say. "Dragon's Eye Peak is a volcano!"

"You mean one of those mountains that blows

up?" asks Barnaby.

You don't answer. You hear something, and it sounds like water running somewhere nearby. It gives you an idea.

"And do you know what makes volcanoes blow up?" you ask as you pull yourself out of the small shaft opening and begin to make your way cautiously along a narrow ledge that runs above the lava.

"No, what?" asks Barnaby, following.

"Pressure!"

You come to an iron gate in the wall. Next to it is a valve with a large wheel. "I hear water on the other side of this gate," you say.

"I hear it too," Barnaby says. "So what?"

"Do you know what would happen if we opened this gate?"

Barnaby looks at you as if you're crazy. "You'd . . . dump water in the lava and make a lot of steam?"

"That's right," you say, beginning to turn the wheel. "Enough steam, hopefully, to make this volcano explode. Just like blowing the top off a pot!"

"You *are* crazy. What good will that do?"

"Do you know any other way to stop the attack?"

The bottom of the gate splits open a crack, and a stream of water trickles through. You give the wheel another turn, and the trickle becomes a torrent!

The water flows into the lava, and you hear a loud hiss. Clouds of vapor billow toward the roof of the cave. You crank the valve all the way open.

"Let's get out of here!" you shout.

The two of you scramble back into the shaft and begin to shinny up. You reach the chamber above just as it's beginning to fill with steamy vapor. You rush out the door and up the tunnels to the main level of the Ayrie.

The vapor is already here, hanging in the air like a dense fog. The council room doors have been thrown open, and the dragons are pouring out, coughing and beating their wings.

You speed through the enormous hallways, until you find what you are looking for: the huge doors that lead out to the mountainside. You dash by the chimera sentry before it has a chance to sound the alarm.

Only when you're well down the mountain do you stop and turn around. The top of the mountain is billowing great clouds of steam, like an overheated teakettle. As you watch, an enormous explosion rips the air. The mountain quakes beneath your feet for several seconds, and the two of you hide under the shelter of an overhanging rock to protect yourselves from a shower of debris.

Some time later, you look out and decide it's safe enough to make the journey home.

"I guess that ends the threat from the dragons," says Barnaby as you tramp along.

"Yes," you say, "but it would have been better if we could have all learned to live in peace. Bosporus wasn't a bad dragon. There may have been others like him."

"You're right," sighs Barnaby. "When we get home, let's ask Father if we can move away from the village. I don't think I'll ever feel comfortable farming on the dragons' nesting grounds."

"That's a good idea." You put your arm around your brother and start the long journey down the mountain.

Not so fast, you two!" you say. "Let's give the Old Man a chance."

Barnaby turns around, looking sheepish, but Finn is obviously irritated. He lugs the heavy book back to the bookshelf and angrily slams it back in place.

"It's a mistake, I'm telling you," he says.

In a few minutes, the Old Man returns. Towering above you, he says, "I've decided to grant your request."

"How sweet!" Finn says, his voice dripping with sarcasm.

You wish he wouldn't say things like that. You're afraid he's going to make the old wizard angry.

"Thank you very much, sir," you say to the Old Man.

"Would you be so kind as to stand there by the door, with your friends?" the Old Man asks, glaring at Finn.

"Why, slay me!" says Finn, hopping across the floor to join you. "You'd think we were all getting married, you would, and he was performing the service."

The Old Man selects a book from an upper shelf, takes it over to the desk, opens it, and for a moment stands over it, reading. Then he begins to speak. The words make no sense to you, but as you listen, you notice the walls of the room are growing misty.

An invisible force draws you out of the Old Man's study. You can only assume the same thing is happening to the others.

Before you completely dematerialize, you catch a glimpse through the mist into the adjoining room, the one where the Old Man disappeared before announcing his decision. To your horror, you see a dragon crouched against the door—a red dragon!

Clyto! you think. The red dragon who killed Bosporus in the mountains near the village!

The Old Man has obviously deceived you. Finn was right. You never should have trusted the wizard. But it's too late now!

Slowly the Old Man's chamber melts away, to be replaced by a new landscape, one of rocks and craggy peaks and howling winds.

"Where are we?" you shout to Barnaby over the wind.

"From the looks of those peaks, I'd say it's Bald Man's Mountain."

"Bald Man's Mountain? But that's miles from where we wanted to be!"

"Aye. Meanwhile, the dragons are mounting their attack."

You throw down your pack, the one containing the gold dragon's claw. You realize it's useless now. You'll never reach the dragons or the village in time.

"Come on," you say to Barnaby and Finn. "We've got a long walk home."

THE END

B arnaby, we've got to go," you say. "If we go back to the village, we might win the battle, but this way we can win the war. It's a risk worth taking."

"All right," he says with a sigh. "If we're going, we're going."

You resume climbing the big dragon's chest. The wounds the red dragon inflicted on the gold's underbelly are so large that they serve as footholds, but they feel squishy under your feet. The sensation makes you a little sick.

"Just how are we going to get to the Ayrie by dawn?" asks Barnaby.

"I have an idea," you say. "We have to find the Old Man of the Mountain."

"The Old Man of the Mountain?" Barnaby echoes. "That crazy geezer?"

"We need magic if we hope to get to the Ayrie in time," you say, "and he's the only wizard we know." You reach the dragon's forefoot and begin to saw through the tough talon.

"But he's so unpredictable. Besides, Father suspects he does magic with the undead. Remember? He said the Old Man smelled of sulfur and rotted flesh."

You remember your father's face the night he came back from the Old Man's retreat. It was as white as chalk, and his eyes were more frightened than you'd ever seen them.

"There's something evil about that wizard," your father said. "I never want to have to see him again." And you know your father never would have gone in the first place if the oxen hadn't been in danger of dying.

You saw through the last bit of the claw. It's almost like cutting a fingernail, but it's as thick as your arm. It's also bleeding a little. "The Old Man helped us before in an emergency. I'm hoping he'll help us again," you declare.

"Well, I don't trust him," says Barnaby. "And I know Father doesn't either. What if he sics a zombie on us?"

"You've never met the Old Man, and Father isn't here," you say. "The Old Man is our only chance."

You jump back to the ground. The claw is dripping blood in big round spots. You hold it gingerly by the sharp end and place it on a rock. Once the claw is drained, you place it between the two dragon scales in your pack and tie the pack up tight. Then you secure the pack and hoist it to your shoulders.

"Time to go," you say.

Barnaby shoulders his own pack with another sigh and falls in behind you for the short hike out of the canyon. You don't mean to be hard on him, but he can be so stubborn, and he tends to make up his mind without knowing all the facts. You just hope he understands how important the quest is.

At the canyon's mouth, you come to the river and follow it into a glade of pines. The sun is hidden in the branches here, and the shade feels cool.

In a short time, you leave the river and begin the long trek across the marshy flats. There are no trees here, only grasses that sway well over your heads. In the tall tufts, the trail narrows to a footpath.

You can't see anything on either side of the trail as it unfolds in front of you. This is a wild animal track, you remember. Anything could be coming around a corner at you at any minute.

A sound up ahead makes you start. You turn and grab Barnaby's arm, your heart pumping. Your brother has heard it too. He stares up the trail, his eyes wide.

Without a word, the two of you leave the path and slip in among the tall grass until you're well hidden.

In a few minutes, you begin to hear voices and the creaking of wagon wheels. Peering out, you realize you know the people coming down the path: Theron Youngblood, a friend of your father's, and some of the men who frequent the Wild Boar Tavern.

"Theron!" Barnaby shouts as he leaps out onto the path in front of the procession.

"Barnaby?" Theron says as Barnaby runs up to him. Theron is a few years younger than your father and always, it seems, in high spirits.

Rats! you think. The last thing we need now is a delay. You decide to rid yourself of these people as soon as possible and you step into view beside your brother.

"Tory?" Theron says. "What are you two doing out here? It's a long way back to the village."

"We might ask you the same thing," you say. "Why aren't you and your friends down at the Wild Boar, as usual?"

Theron grins. "Why, we're hunting dragons, of course! See?" He points back to a wagon drawn by two tired-looking horses. Mounted on the wagon is a large catapult.

"So are we," says Barnaby. "Actually, we're after scales."

"Way out here? You'll never make it back home before nightfall."

"We don't intend to," you say. "We plan to camp out."

"We were just about to make camp ourselves," says Theron. "Would you like to join us?"

"No, thanks," you say hastily. "We've still got some ground to cover. We want to get as far as White Stone Wash. There's good scale hunting there we hear."

You turn to find Barnaby glaring at you. Apparently the thought of a borrowed bedroll and a warm meal appealed to him.

"We wouldn't mind having a little something to eat, though," Barnaby says. "We left in such a hurry this morning, we forgot half our supplies."

"Why, of course!" Theron turns to the others. "Spread out, boys. We can camp right here." As Theron's men are unpacking their supplies and making a fire, Barnaby pulls you aside. "Now's our chance to warn the village," he whispers. "We can tell Theron about the dragon attack tomorrow, and he can bring word back to the others."

"What happens when Theron finds out about the dangerous mission we're on?" you ask. "What if he won't let us go? He might think he's doing us a favor by protecting us."

"You have a point there," Barnaby admits. "Fine, I won't say anything, but if we don't stop the attack and the whole village goes up in flames, it's on your head."

Your brother's words strike at your heart. What should you do? Should you give the village a fair warning and run the risk of having Theron try to stop you? Or should you keep quiet and slip away from the party of hunters as soon as possible?

If you want to tell your story to Theron and the others and ask them to warn the village, turn to page 78.

turn to page 78.

72

If you think it would be safer not to tell them, turn to page 135.

turn to page 135.

You decide you've got to hide, or you may not be around long enough to rescue your brother. Before dashing behind the rock, you take a quick glance over the ledge. By some miracle, the rope has tangled around Barnaby's arm. He's unconscious and dangling from it, some eighty feet below.

You turn and run to the rock where Finn is hiding. I hope Barnaby will be all right for the time being, you think.

BOOM! BOOM! The noises sound like heavy footfalls. They're coming from behind the door. Peering out from behind the rock, you see the handle move, and you hold your breath as the door swings open with a loud creak.

A head emerges—a *huge* head, as large as a wagon, with a thick crop of unruly, green hair.

"It's the Storm Giant's wife!" whispers Finn.

"Is she friendly?" you ask.

"Hard to say. Best we wait and see."

"What's all the racket down here?" Her voice, so loud it makes you tremble, booms in the cavern. "If it's another one of you confounded wererats, you'll be sorry!" she continues.

She steps out of the room onto the ledge, the force of her enormous feet sending vibrations through the stone, until she's right over you.

You feel eerie being so close to a body so large—the smells, the sight of her green flesh, the huge strands of hair.

"What's this?" the Storm Giantess mutters. "Someone's broken the old bridge." She steps to the edge of the rock ledge. "Well, what have we here?" she says, stooping down.

Carefully, she draws up the severed rope, with Barnaby hanging from the end like a fish on a fish line.

"Poor little thing," she murmurs, examining Barnaby. "I'd better take you inside."

No! you think. You're ready to risk everything to stop her, but before you can move, she's turned and disappeared back through the huge door.

"Come on!" you say. "We've got to rescue Barnaby!"

The giantess has left the door open a crack, and you and Finn slip inside, climb up the broad stone steps, and enter the largest kitchen you've ever seen.

The huge woman is standing in the center of the kitchen, examining Barnaby intently in the light of an overhead lantern.

"Hmm. Nothing seems to be broken. What a handsome little fellow! Won't his lordship be surprised to see you?"

You and Finn press yourselves back against the wall near the bottom of the cupboard.

"On the other hand, his lordship ate my last house pet," the giantess goes on. "Confuses easily. Maybe we won't tell him about you. What do you say to that, little fellow? Would you like to be my little secret?"

She pulls up a chair that you guess must be twelve feet high and sits at a table that's bigger than your house, placing Barnaby on the tabletop in front of her. Then she positions her two great elbows, one on either side of Barnaby, and leans forward to watch him.

You crouch down to Finn's level. "We'll never be able to get Barnaby away from her now," you whisper. "We never should have come here."

"Patience, my friend, patience. Remember, it's *her* husband we've come to see. But hush!"

"What a little cutie!" coos the giantess. "I'll make sure his lordship never eats you. He probably won't even notice you, he's so busy with those dragons, keeping the weather clear for their attack in the morning. Him and his dragons! Why he associates with those smelly things, I'll never understand. Ever since he got involved in their attack, it's do this, do that! You'd think he was the Old Man of the Mountain the way he tries to order me about!"

You can scarcely believe what she's saying! The Storm Giant in cahoots with the dragons? You glare furiously at Finn.

The little man shrugs sheepishly. "It's been a while, it has, since I've had news of the Storm Giant. Maybe he's changed his views."

"He'd listen to us, that's what you said," you whisper. "How can we ask him to help us stop the attack when he's helping the dragons with it?"

"It's a sad thing, but even we leprechauns occasionally make mistakes."

Your mind is racing, trying to think of another plan.

"The Storm Giant will never be any help to us," you say. "We've got to rescue Barnaby and get out of here."

"You know, she's not such a bad egg," says Finn, nodding toward the Storm Giantess. "Maybe she'd be willing to help."

You give the huge woman a thoughtful look. Finn could be right. She certainly seems to be kind. Then again, there's nothing to say she won't keep all three of you as pets. Once again, it looks like you're going to have to make a decision.

> If you decide to take a chance and reveal your presence to the giantess, turn to page 123.

> If you prefer to wait and try to rescue Barnaby, then make your escape, turn to page 114.

Barnaby's warning that the fate of your village is "on your head" convinces you. He's right, you think. We really have to warn the village about the attack.

You walk back to where Theron is directing the setting up of the camp. "There's something I have to tell you, Theron," you say.

You tell the entire story, leaving out nothing. The other hunters gather around, drawn by your story. When you show them the dragon's claw stuffed deep in your pack, you can tell they are convinced.

"The villagers have to be warned as soon as possible," Theron says. He turns to one of the young men. "Take one of the horses. Ride to the village and sound the alarm. We'll wait here with the catapult."

The young man leaps on his mount and rides off into the night. You watch him go, and when he's out of sight, you turn to Theron.

"You can see now why we can't stay. Barnaby and I have to get to the Ayrie. We have to convince the dragons that peace has already been made."

"I've been thinking about that," he says. "It seems pretty dangerous for a couple of kids like you to be traveling in the mountains at night. It's too risky to let you go."

This is exactly what you were afraid of. You try to cut him off by saying, "Maybe it is risky, but I promised the dragon I'd try!"

"Take it easy, Tory! I didn't mean for you to get upset," Theron says.

"I'm not upset," you say. "I'm just saying we're going, that's all. Barnaby, get your pack."

Suddenly you feel strong hands grab you by the elbows. One of Theron's friends has grabbed you from behind, and you can't turn around.

Barnaby quickly sees what's happening and comes running up. "Hey! What do you think you're doing? Let go!"

But Theron slips around behind him and pins his arms behind his back. They push you both over to the wagon and force you to sit by the wheel. Then they tie your hands behind you to the spokes.

"Why are you doing this?" your brother asks, pulling against the ropes.

"It's for your own good," Theron says, squatting beside you. "We can't let you two go on a quest like that. It's too dangerous. Besides, I owe it to your father. I know you two—especially you, Tory. You'd go however dangerous it was. We'll untie you in the morning. Meanwhile, you might as well get some rest."

When he's gone, you turn to Barnaby. "Next time I tell you we're leaving, we leave right then," you say.

"It's not my fault," says Barnaby, trying to shrug despite having his hands tied. "I didn't know Theron would tie us up. And I tried to save you."

You're about to reply when you notice a movement in the shadows near the back of the wagon. Your pack is lying on the ground nearby, and something is stealing toward it.

"Hey, you! Stop!" you shout.

The figure stops and stares at you. It's a little man, not more than two feet high and dressed in the most outlandish costume you've ever seen. His clothes are bright green, cut to resemble leaves. On his feet are two bright green boots with toes that curl up into points. Atop his head is a piece of birch bark, rolled into a cone and tied with a leather strap.

"A leprechaun!" Barnaby whispers. "Don't take your eyes off of it!"

You remember the stories you've heard about the wee folk ever since you were a child. It's said that if you take your eyes off a leprechaun even for a second, the tiny creature will vanish.

You widen your eyes, determined not to blink as you stare at the little figure. "Come here, you little thief! Stay away from that bundle!"

The little man looks at you, a sheepish grin playing at the corners of his tiny mouth.

"Now, what could you want with old Finn?" he asks.

"What do you want with my bundle?"

"Your bundle, is it? And here I thought it was just left there for the taking." He looks over your shoulder. "Say—is that a bugbear creeping up on you?"

You know the leprechaun is trying to make you look away so he can vanish, but you really could use his help. You've heard that if you plead with a leprechaun and your cause is just, he has no choice but to help you. And once in your power, the tiny creature is bound to your service forever. You keep your eyes locked on him.

"Do you know what's in that bundle?" you ask.

"Gold, maybe?" asks the little man hopefully.

"A dragon's claw," you say.

82

"Imagine that! The foreclaw of some vile, leather-hided beast. Why, run me through with a stake!"

"Would you like to know why I have a dragon's claw in my pack?" you ask.

"Tell him about the dragon fight, Tory!" says Barnaby.

"A story I shouldn't miss, is it?" the leprechaun says. "An amusing anecdote guaranteed to entertain?"

"Absolutely," you say. "Come a little closer, and I'll tell you."

You can see that the leprechaun doesn't want to obey you, but you stare at him unwaveringly, and he can't seem to resist. The little man inches in your direction.

You relate the story of the dying dragon and the tale it told you, just as you did with Theron.

"So you see what we're up against," you conclude. "We've got to reach the Ayrie by dawn and convince the dragons there's no need to attack. Then we can begin working out arrangements to move off our land."

A sparkling tear rolls out of the corner of the little man's eye and trickles down his green face. "As touching a tale as I've ever heard," he says with a sigh. "And urgent too. I suppose you'll be wanting my help now?"

"We could use a hand getting out of these ropes," you say.

"And please be quick about it!" puts in Barnaby. "Theron could come back any minute."

"Well, it's a grand tale, indeed. A regular drama. And I can see it's the truth you're telling me, too, and I thank you for that. But I have to say to myself, Finn, I say, after all these years, you've finally been caught by one of the big folk. Have you finally met your destiny?"

A footfall sounds near the fire, and a shadow falls on the grass not far away.

"Are you trying to get caught twice in one night, little man? Untie these ropes! He's coming!" Barnaby says.

Quickly the little leprechaun slips behind the wagon wheel. You feel his deft fingers working the knots, and the ropes loosen.

"Think of it!" whispers the little man. "After all these centuries of freedom, I've finally met my destiny!"

The ropes abruptly give way, and your hands are free. You snatch up the bundle while Finn loosens Barnaby's hands, then the three of you slip into the tall grass.

You hear Theron's shouts as you speed through the foliage, but soon they're no more than echoes fading in the distance behind you.

Up ahead, you see a single scrub pine sticking its branches out of the marsh. The three of you stop beside it to rest.

"So, my friends, what's the plan?" pants the leprechaun, plopping down on a tree root, one little hand on either thigh as he tries to catch his breath. "Some grand and clever plot to get us to the Ayrie just in the nick of time? Swashbuckling the guards? Beguiling the monsters?"

"We're on our way to see the Old Man of the Mountain," you reply. You cast your eyes skyward. You realize that it's getting late. The sun has already begun to set. You wasted far too much time with Theron.

"The Old Man of the Mountain? Why, he's an evil magician, he is. You don't want to be seeing him. Not at night, especially."

"But we need some kind of a spell to transport us to the Ayrie," you say. "It's the only way we'll ever get there in time."

"Aye, a spell! Good thinking there. But the Old Man of the Mountain? I should think it'd be the Storm Giant you'd be wanting to see. Now, there's a creature with some love in his heart. He'd listen to your tale of woe, he would. But the Old Man? Ooo!" says the leprechaun, wrinkling his nose. "A cold fish, that one."

The leprechaun's suggestion catches you off guard. You've never heard of the Storm Giant. You know about the Old Man of the Mountain. However, your father called him evil and swore he'd never go back. But the Storm Giant intrigues you. Should you abandon the plan to see the Old Man and go to the Storm Giant instead?

Whatever you decide, you should decide quickly. The day is growing short and it will be dark before you reach the mountains.

If you decide to seek out the
Old Man of the Mountain,
turn to page 108.

turn to page 108.

86

If you elect to take the
leprechaun's advice and get
help from the Storm Giant,
turn to page 96.

turn to page 96.

You think about carrying Finn back out through the rugged mountains, and you wonder if it would work. As you look at the little leprechaun, you see what Barnaby said is true. If anything, Finn is growing weaker. He looks paler and more tired now than he was an hour ago.

Perhaps the darkness and stale air of this underground passageway has something to do with it. Maybe if you got him out of here, he'd start to feel better.

Carefully you put one hand under his small head and the other beneath his knees.

"Come on, Finn. We're going to get out of here and go someplace where you can breathe. Barnaby, grab my pack."

"This is stupid," says Barnaby, shaking his head. "You aren't thinking about the village!"

"Bless you, my friend," says Finn as you hoist him up.

Outside, everything is still dark, but the night has definitely grown later. The moon has turned orange and sits close to the horizon.

"We'll never make it now," Barnaby says. "The village is doomed!"

The little man feels like a broken doll in your arms as you carry him down the path, past the rock where you hid from the wererats, past the

sharp turn where you sent them plunging over the cliff.

You carry Finn to a point well away from the Old Man's lair, while Barnaby follows moodily, both packs hoisted on his back.

On a bed of soft dirt, well out in the open where the air is fresh, you set the little fellow down. Joyfully you note that his color is improving, and his lips, which had been ashen before, now have some of their old pinkness back.

"It's a brave thing you've done, my friends," the leprechaun murmurs gratefully. "A grand, brave thing. Gather round me. There's something I want to say."

Barnaby moves in close, next to where you kneel over the little man.

"You two have sacrificed a great deal for me, you have. You gave up a chance to save your village to save me instead."

"Maybe we never really had a chance to save the village," you say.

"Now, now. None of that. No one will ever know. But I'm grateful to you, I am. And I want to repay you. I'm a rich leprechaun, though you wouldn't know it to look at me. I've a treasure, I have, a fortune in hidden gold. I want you to take it. Give it to the villagers who lose their homes. You may not be able to save your village, but at least you can soften the blow."

"Oh wow!" Barnaby says. "We'll take it."

"That's generous of you, Finn," you add, patting the little fellow gently on the hand.

"But now begone, you two. Never mind me. I'll recover and return to wandering, just like before. But if you don't hurry, you won't reach the village by daylight in time to warn them, and many lives will be lost. No treasure in the world is worth even one life. Go on, now. Forget about those silly dragons. You can tell them later their attack was foolish and unnecessary."

"You want us to just leave you like this?" you ask.

"Yes! Just go! Now! Quick as rabbits! You've a lot of ground to cover by daybreak. Here, take this map," he says, reaching into his shirt and producing a small, faded piece of parchment. He presses it into your hand. "That shows where the treasure's hidden. But hurry, now!"

And so you say goodbye to your little friend and hurry off down the mountain with your brother, thinking what a remarkable adventure this has been—strange and magical, and still far from over.

And yet in the end, you think, I'm sure it'll all come out all right.

You're sure you can cast the spell and do it right, Finn?" you ask.

"Aye," he says, "as sure as there's a pot of gold at the end of the rainbow."

"All right, then, let's go."

But no sooner has Finn hoisted the book onto his shoulder than the doorknob rattles. The Old Man's coming back!

In a panic, you and Barnaby start for the door leading to the outside.

"Not that way!" Finn whispers. "He'll look for us there. This way! Quickly!"

Finn scampers up a winding stone staircase, and you and Barnaby follow.

You burst into what looks like some kind of observation room. In the far wall is a slitlike window that looks out on the valley below.

Finn's little eyes search the room. "Slay me! Not an exit in sight! They've bottled us like flies in a jar, they have!"

Downstairs, you hear the Old Man's voice. "After them, my pets! Pick them apart with your teeth!"

You look at Barnaby, and he looks back at you.

"Wererats!" he says.

Sure enough, in a moment you hear the patter of dozens of padded feet on the stairway.

"This way!" Finn says. He heaves the book out the slitlike window, then tries to get a leg up on the sill himself. Quickly you give him a boost and follow after him as he tumbles out onto the rocks below.

Fortunately it isn't a sheer drop. You land on your feet, stoop to grab the book, and keep on running.

But the wererats have spotted you. Their dim shapes fill the window as they scramble after you.

"They're catching up!" shouts Barnaby.

You glance back and see that he's right. The wererats are gaining. You'll have to think of something!

Up ahead, Finn disappears over a stony rise. When you top the same rise, the little man leaps out, grabs your leg, and pulls you to a stop.

You look down and see why. You're standing on a narrow ledge several hundred feet above a rushing river. Another two steps and you'd have gone over.

In the nick of time, you reach out and grab Barnaby and stop him too. The two of you stand looking at the water swirling in the moonlight far below. You both realize how close you came to going over the ledge.

Then you remember the wererats.

Without a second to lose, you tear the pack from your back and pull out your last dragon scale. Turning it shiny side up, you dash back to the top of the rise.

The wererats have scattered now, and are combing the rocks, giving out puzzled, anxious squeaks. Apparently they lost you when you disappeared from view. You hold the scale up high and wave it at them.

The scale acts just like a magnet to the wererats. As you hurry back to the ledge, they race over the rise at full speed, their whiskered mouths wide open in agonized screams as they plunge over the cliff to the river below, their hands desperately clawing the air as they fall to their deaths.

Finn whistles as the last of them disappears into the white water. "That was a bit of luck. But we've work to do, my friends."

He shoulders the spellbook and begins edging along the narrow ledge that borders the cliff.

Half an hour later, you find yourself trudging across a rocky flat with the Aliwar Range towering in the distance.

"When are you going to work your spell?" you say. You've asked Finn the same question half a dozen times already, but he keeps putting you off. Your patience is at an end. "Every second we waste, the dawn gets closer. We can't afford to wait much longer."

"I agree with Tory," Barnaby puts in. "Let's get on with it . . . Wait a minute," he says, pointing upward. "What's that?"

You follow his finger and see lights shining near the top of a nearby mountain. It looks as though fires are burning in a cave somewhere high in the cliff face.

"The Ayrie, I'll warrant!" says the leprechaun.

"Why, I'll bet we could walk there!" Barnaby says. "It can't be that far!"

"The mountains play tricks on your eyes, there. It's still a pretty piece. But we're out of range of the Old Man's magic now. It's time to do a bit of spellcasting."

The little man plunks down on a nearby rock

and begins reading his book. Meanwhile, Barnaby draws you aside.

"This plan scares me," he whispers. "I was all for using the magic book back when it was a choice between that and the Old Man, but now I'm not so sure. If we can make it to the Ayrie on foot, why risk a spell? Remember how it felt to be turned into ghosts?"

You look once more at the lights at the top of the mountain in the distance. It's difficult to judge how far away they are or even how much time is left before dawn. On the other hand, Finn's spell may well be dangerous. He said he didn't have the ability to send you to the Ayrie, but now, armed only with the Old Man's spellbook, he's about to try. What should you do?

If you choose to let Finn cast his spell, turn to page 19.

If you trust Barnaby's judgment and decide to walk to the Ayrie, turn to page 156.

Y ou decide to give Finn's suggestion a try and
go see the Storm Giant for help. Leaving
the marsh, you allow the little fellow to take the
lead.

He follows a meandering path into the foothills, and after several hours of what seems to be
aimless wandering, your patience is at an end.

"When will we get to the Storm Giant's
castle?" you ask, making no attempt to hide your
irritation.

"It can't be much farther now, my friend,"
Finn says. "That is, if my old mixed-up brain
hasn't deceived me."

"It better not have," says Barnaby.

In a gorge just ahead, you hear a metallic
clanking sound, and on the rock face of the gorge
you can see the flickering reflection of a fire.

Well, he's led us to something, you think,
although you doubt it's the Storm Giant.

You round a rocky outcropping and see
a stone house standing just off the path. In
front of it, a small man is digging with a pick
and shovel. He's very old, and a pointed white
beard hangs down to his belly. Finn motions

for the two of you to draw near.

"He's a dwarf," Finn whispers. "They're a hard-working lot and friendly enough. I'll ask him the way to the Storm Giant's castle."

The dwarf may be small, but Finn looks like a toddler as he goes forth with a happy wave of his walking stick and attracts the dwarf's attention. The two talk for several minutes, then Finn turns back to you, a disturbed look on his face.

"I've got bad news for you. It's the wrong trail we've been following. The Storm Giant's castle lies several leagues in the other direction. Old Finn, I'm afraid, has muddled it."

What are you going to do now? Emotions crowd in on you so fast you can hardly take stock of them. You sit down on the trail, your hand to your forehead, trying to sort them out.

Barnaby, however, is nothing but angry. "You little trickster! We've wasted hours following you around this mountain. Now we'll never make it to the Ayrie in time!"

"Excuse me," says the dwarf, stepping forward modestly. "The leprechaun told me you have to reach Dragon's Eye Peak by dawn in order to prevent an attack on your village?"

"That's right," you say, "but we need magic or some kind of shortcut, or we'll never make it in time!"

"Ah, but I know of such a shortcut," says the dwarf. "Allow me. My name is Oskar. Once, long ago, a clan of my people mined these hills. We dug many tunnels, some of which connect with other tunnels under the Ayrie."

You jump to your feet. "You mean there's an underground shortcut to the Ayrie?" you ask.

"Indeed," says the old dwarf, stroking his beard. "I believe it still is possible to reach the Ayrie before your deadline."

"And you'll show us the way?" asks Barnaby.

"I will. Your cause seems just. But I must warn you, the tunnels have long been abandoned. Every day I hear the rumblings of new cave-ins, and what kinds of creatures are living down there now, no one can guess."

"Aha!" Finn shouts, dancing a jig. "You see, my friends, the luck of the leprechauns is a grand thing, it is. Old Finn led you astray, only to stumble on a better find. To the tunnels, I say!"

"What do you think, Tory?" Barnaby asks, looking dubious. "Should we try it?"

"I don't really know," you say. "There's still time to go back and see the Old Man of the Mountain. I just don't know which to choose."

But you'll have to make up your mind, and quickly. Every minute wasted brings you closer to dawn and the destruction of your village. Which will it be—Oskar's tunnels or the Old Man of the Mountain?

If you choose to try the dwarf's shortcut, turn to page 16.

If you elect to backtrack to see the Old Man of the Mountain, turn to page 37.

arnaby, we don't even know where Aurea is," you say. "In fact, chances are good that she's inside that chamber. Finn said justice would prevail, and justice is on our side. I think a direct approach is best."

"But, Tory—"

You refuse to listen. Armed with Bosporus's claw on your back, you step out from behind the pillar, in full view of the chimera.

All three heads react with total astonishment. As you come closer, the dragon head extends itself forward and peers at you in disbelief.

"A human!" it says.

"From the village, no doubt," adds the lion head.

"Inform the council at once!" the goat head says.

"Wait! I'm here as a friend," you say, trying to calm them down. "I bring a message from Bosporus."

"Bosporus?" the lion repeats.

"Inform the council!" the dragon head says. "Clyto will know what to do!"

By this time, Barnaby, too, has ventured out from behind the pillar.

"Another human!" the goat shouts. "It's an

invasion! Quick! Tell Clyto!"

"Clyto?" you say. "Oh no!" The double doors fly open with a bang. Behind them is a gathering of many dragons, seated not on chairs but on perches mounted at various heights on the wall. On the floor, apparently addressing the assemblage, is the red dragon who attacked Bosporus back in the valley by your village. When he sees you, he hurries out and slams the doors behind him.

"What's going on here?" he demands.

All the chimera's heads begin talking at once.

"We're being invaded!" cries the goat.

"He says he has a message," the lion says.

"From Bosporus," adds the dragon.

"A message from Bosporus? In the hands of a human?" Clyto stares down at you.

You look up into Clyto's glowing eyes, and suddenly your knees feel weak. You realize you've made a terrible mistake. This is Bosporus's enemy. Without thinking, you've delivered yourself right into his hands!

"Come with me. Quickly!" he says to you, then turns to the chimera. "Give my apologies to the council. I will return shortly," he says, then leads the two of you away.

He ushers you to a nearby room, which has been furnished for dragons. A perch extends out from the wall, and on the floor is a nest of pine boughs and ferns. Clyto makes sure the door is locked, then settles himself on the nest.

"Fools," he says harshly. "You've stumbled into something you know nothing about! Don't bother to tell me Bosporus is dead. I should know. I killed him. And don't tell me about the peace agreement either. I have no use for peace! These dragons want war, and I'm going to give it to them. And when I do, I will be declared ruler!"

He pauses to eye you both carefully. A profound fear fills you, deeper than any fear you've ever felt. It's going to take a miracle to get you out of this alive.

"I'm not exactly sure how to dispose of you," the red dragon goes on matter-of-factly. "I could roast you over the Eternal Fires. Or I could take you back to the council meeting and expose you as spies. That might be politically useful. I could always kill you later. Of course, there would be risks, but then there are always risks. On the other hand"—a cruel smile curls the ends of his long, serpentine mouth—"maybe I'll just leave the choice up to you. Which do you prefer?"

What will you answer? How do you make a choice between two kinds of death?

If you tell Clyto you'd prefer to be taken before the council and exposed as spies, turn to page 188.

If you say instead that you'd prefer to be roasted, turn to page 57.

One of the ghosts lunges toward you, its mouth a gaping, screaming hole. You duck back among the rocks with a shudder.

"Let's try that tunnel of yours," you say to Finn.

"Right you are! Any wizard who keeps rats and ghosts at his door isn't one to be helping us much, I'm afraid."

One by one, the three of you dash for the tunnel. The walls are cold and damp, but it isn't until you're well inside that you realize you forgot to bring a torch for a light.

"Allow me," says Finn. The little man snaps his fingers, and they begin to glow. The soft light provides enough light to keep you from stumbling.

"Not bad," you say.

"Oh, if I were a real wizard, I'd light you a light you'd never forget, I would. I'd turn these very walls to light, and they'd glow with all the colors of the rainbow. But alas, I'm only a humble leprechaun."

"Well, a leprechaun, anyway," says Barnaby.

You and your brother share a smile. You

have to admit, you're becoming rather fond of the little fellow.

For more than an hour, you trudge through the narrow confines of the tunnel as it leads you down through the mountain. As you go, the air becomes danker, the walls more moist. Finally, up ahead, you hear a sound. At first you think it must be a large crowd of creatures talking, and for a brief second, you think you've finally reached the Ayrie. But as you get closer, you recognize the sound as the roar of rushing water.

A few feet farther on, the tunnel ends abruptly in an enormous cavern. Below is a sheer drop of more than a hundred feet, ending in a raging river that surges across the cavern floor, making a terrible racket. The river must be magical, because every now and then it flashes with an eerie blue light that illuminates the entire chamber.

Extending from the opening across the chasm is a dilapidated bridge, so old that most of the planks have fallen off. On the other side of the chamber, in the cavern's far wall, is another opening, in which you see an enormous wooden door. The door is closed.

"This is it, my friends," Finn calls out when he sees the cavern. "The Storm Giant's rooms are just beyond that door!"

"You're not suggesting we cross this bridge, are you?" Barnaby asks. "It looks like it's about to collapse."

"Nonsense!" Finn says, springing onto the rope handhold and crossing the yawning chasm like a tightrope walker. "Safe as can be," he calls back as he jumps to the ledge on the far side.

Barnaby looks at you doubtfully, wondering whether to follow. Then he shrugs and starts to mount the rickety bridge. The support posts begin to groan. He jumps back.

"Wait a minute, Barnaby," you say. "Let's think this over."

But what's the alternative? you wonder. You must either cross the bridge, or forget about the Stone Giant altogether and go back up the tunnel to the Old Man of the Mountain. There's no reason to think that the situation there would be any different now. You'd still have the ghosts to contend with, and there's no guarantee that the Old Man would be willing to help. In addition, you have lost valuable time.

You don't want to go back there, but the bridge looks like it's going to fall apart any minute. You shake your head. What are you going to do?

> ✦ **If you attempt to cross the bridge, turn to page 143.**

> ✦ **If you decide to retrace your steps up the tunnel to the Old Man of the Mountain, turn to page 169.**

You were right to suspect it would be night-fall by the time you reached the Old Man of the Mountain's sanctuary. The doorway is built into the side of the mountain itself. Outlined in the moonlight, the passage is no more than a dark hole in the mountainside.

You, Barnaby, and Finn creep up as close as you dare and conceal yourselves behind a rock that overlooks the passage.

Barnaby's hands are shaking like leaves. You look at your own, and to your surprise, they're shaking too.

"You're right to be frightened," Finn whispers. "A practitioner of the dark arts draws the creatures of night around him like a cloak."

The wind carries the sound of gnawing from the passageway.

"What's that?" asks Barnaby.

"Wererats," says Finn. "Part rat, part human. They hang about the Old Man's door waiting for the leftovers from his fiendish experiments."

"Yuck!" says Barnaby.

"Shhh!" Finn hisses.

A long, rodentlike head pokes out through the

opening into the moonlight. Its ears and whiskers twitch as it sniffs the night air.

"It's looking for us," whispers Finn in a voice so quiet you can hardly hear it.

For several seconds the wererat lingers, then as quickly as it came, it withdraws.

"It didn't see us!" Barnaby says, sounding relieved.

"Aye, but the wererats will discover us eventually," says Finn. "It's only a matter of time."

"Finn's right," you say. "We have to think of some way to distract the wererats."

"It looks just like a big rat. But with hands," Barnaby says. "Too bad we don't have a giant piece of cheese. Or a giant cat. I bet a giant cat would scare it."

"Just like a rat . . ." you say. "Here, Barnaby, help me off with this pack. I've got an idea."

Finn climbs on top of the rock and keeps watch while you and Barnaby take off your pack and unlace it. You pull out one of the dragon scales you found earlier.

"Now give me your belt, Barnaby."

"Do you have any idea what you're doing?" he asks, undoing the double length of rope he uses to hold up his pants.

"I'm getting rid of an obstacle," you say, taking out your knife. "Now help me punch a hole in this dragon scale."

Between the two of you, you manage to whittle an opening in the tough scale large enough to insert the rope. Then you tie a knot on the other side of the hole. Finally you tuck the scale and the rope under your arm and get up.

"Tory," whispers Barnaby. "Be careful."

"Don't worry. Now listen, you two. When you see the rats come out, you run in and knock on the door. The Old Man will answer."

"What if he doesn't let us in?" asks Barnaby.

"Tell him you're from the village and need help. He'll probably be annoyed, but he'll let you in."

"Good luck, Tory."

"Aye, may the luck of the leprechauns be with you," Finn says.

"Thanks," you say. "I'll need it."

A narrow rock ledge extends above the path leading to the entrance of the passageway. You climb onto it and begin inching your way toward the passage opening.

You pause to loop the rope around your neck, so the dragon scale hangs behind you. The scale is so shiny that it almost glows in the dark. You're going to hate to lose it.

Step by step, you make your way along the ledge, being careful not to knock dust or pebbles onto the path. Finally you reach a tiny shelf overlooking the dark hole of the passage. Very carefully, you undo the rope and let down the scale, dangling it like a fishing lure in front of the opening.

You hear scratching noises inside the passage. They're coming. Rats are rats the world over. They love shiny objects.

You sense the wererats creeping nearer. You can almost see their beady little eyes watching the scale revolve in the moonlight.

You wait until the last possible minute. Just as you feel they're about to reach for the scale, you leap down onto the path and set off at a run, dragging the scale behind you.

You race as fast as you can, hurdling boulders and leaping over crags that spring up in the dim light.

You can tell the wererats are right behind you. You can hear their wild squeaks and the slap of their bare feet as they try to grab the scale.

You come to the spot you'd noticed earlier as you and your companions were climbing to the sanctuary. The path takes a sharp turn right next to a steep cliff. You race around the corner and stop abruptly, hidden from sight. Then you hurl the scale out into the abyss.

In a mad rush, the wererats dash into empty space, following the scale, then catch themselves on the rocks on the steep slope below and cling there for dear life.

Heaving a sigh of relief, you go back to look for Finn and your brother. You expect to find them inside the Old Man's inner sanctum, but they've encountered yet another obstacle.

"Ghosts!" whispers Finn as you rejoin them in the passageway. "And a fine awful pack of them they are too!"

Your companions have hidden themselves behind a large rock in the passageway. Ahead of them in the darkness, luminous shapes float in the air, their mouths twisted in fleshless grins.

"Oh, I hate ghosts," Barnaby says, his teeth chattering. "They scare me half to death! I want to go back, Tory."

With a tiny finger, Finn beckons the two of you to listen to him. "The way I see it, we've a choice to be making. A tunnel near here leads off to the right. A little voice keeps telling me it's a back door to the Storm Giant's castle, and we could be there in the blink of an eye if we follow it."

"Or we could find a way to get around these ghosts and push on to see the Old Man," you counter. "There's no guarantee that tunnel leads where you say it does, Finn, and even if it does, we don't know if the Storm Giant will help us."

From the look on his face, Barnaby favors the tunnel. He certainly doesn't like the ghosts. Which should you do?

If you want to try the tunnel, turn to page 104.

On the other hand, if you want to tackle the ghosts, turn to page 52.

Finding someone to help you save the village is important, but the Storm Giantess has your brother in immediate danger.

"Let's wait a minute," you whisper. "Maybe something will happen to give us an opening."

Finn nods, and sure enough, it isn't long before you hear a commotion in the next room.

"That would be the Storm Giant, waking up," whispers Finn.

The Giantess hears it too. "I'm coming, dearest," she calls and lumbers out of the kitchen.

Quickly you and Finn climb up onto the table and revive Barnaby. He's a bit groggy, but he seems all right, and he's very glad to see the two of you.

"Come on!" says Finn. "We'll have to make a run for it!"

The three of you scramble off the table to the floor and scamper away. You reach the doorway just as the giantess is coming back in. You press yourself against the wall near the doorjamb.

To your relief, she fails to see you and heads toward the table.

"Where is he?" she thunders when she sees

that Barnaby is gone. "Where's my pet?" She checks under the table.

You realize it's only a matter of time before she sees you. "Run!" you shout to the others.

You fly through the door, with Barnaby and Finn close behind you. But the giantess has spotted you!

"Come back here!" she shouts.

The next room is huge—large even for a giant, mammoth if you're only normal size. You speed through it into yet another room, equally as large, but this one has a door, and you can feel an air current streaming under it.

The giantess's huge feet pound the floor behind you. You don't dare look back, but you know she's got to be close.

The three of you dive under the door at the same time. Finn crawls right through, but you and Barnaby have to squeeze.

You make it just as the huge door swings open above you, and there, outlined against the lights outside, is the Storm Giantess! She reaches for Barnaby, but he slips through her fingers.

"Come back here, you little rascals!" she shouts.

But it's too late. You're already scrambling down the mountain path under the protection of the darkness. She won't find you now.

When you can no longer hear her cries, the three of you regroup under a rocky overhang some distance from the castle.

"Now what?" you ask. "Our visit to the Storm Giant certainly didn't work out."

"I feel personally responsible," says Finn.

"You should!" Barnaby says. "If it hadn't been for you, we'd have gone to the Old Man of the Mountain for help, and we wouldn't be in this mess!"

"It's too late for that now," you say, looking out at the eastern sky. The clouds are already starting to turn pink.

"Well, my friends, seeing as it's the old leprechaun's fault, the old leprechaun will just have to fix it, now won't he? Gather round me."

Finn perches on a rock between you and your brother. You're furious with him, but reluctantly, you turn around to listen.

"I've been keeping an ace up my sleeve, I have, for just such an emergency," he says.

"I knew it was possible—just possible, mind you—that we might not make it to the Ayrie in time, and seeing as we didn't, and that I'm partly to blame, I've decided to part with my most precious possession: my pot of gold. A big one it is, too, the result of years of wandering and collecting. Take the gold and distribute it among the villagers. It'll ease the pain of having to start their lives over."

"Oh!" you say. "That's very generous of you!"

"Good idea, Finn," says Barnaby.

"It's the least I can do," says the leprechaun. "But time's a-wasting, my friends. You'll have to hurry back to the village and warn them. I'll meet you there with the gold after the attack. There'll be plenty for all, I promise you!"

It isn't until later, as you're hurrying down the path toward the village, that you realize a great deal depends on how much you trust Finn.

"What do you think, Barnaby? Do you think Finn will show up?" you ask.

"I hope so," your brother says. "He's not

mean, just scatterbrained. I think he'll keep his promise."

118 You smile, thinking about the good feeling you've had about Finn all along, and what Finn always said about trusting your instincts. You feel sure the little man won't let you down. "Me too," you tell your brother.

It's one of the hardest decisions you've ever had to make, but in the end, the thought of being responsible for dragons roasting your friends and family alive proves too much.

"Maybe you're right, Barnaby. Maybe we should just be thankful we found out about the attack in time. Come on," you say, sheathing your knife and starting back down the mountain. "Let's go warn the village."

The journey home is long and tiring. Even though you move as fast as you can, it's late at night when you and Barnaby trudge through the village gate. The rutted mud path that serves as the main street is deserted, and most of the houses are dark.

Halfway across the town square, you and Barnaby separate. You've already decided that Barnaby will warn the men in the tavern while you'll warn your father and start packing.

Your father is waiting for you as you enter. "Where have you been?" he asks as he struggles to his feet. The warm light of the fire can't disguise the pallor on his face. He hasn't felt well in a long time, but tonight he looks particularly weak.

"We have to get out of here," you say, moving past him. "Now. Tonight."

"What are you talking about?" he asks.

You begin rummaging through the room, pulling open cupboards and drawers, gathering essential items you know you'll want to bring with you.

"I'll explain while we pack, but please hurry. We haven't much time!" you say.

As you continue to gather your things, you tell your father what you learned from the gold dragon. At first he doesn't believe you, but then, sensing your urgency, he begins to pack too.

Two hours later, you've harnessed the horses and filled the wagon with all you own. Your father brings out one last item: a rocking chair he likes to sit in while he watches the sun go down. He hands it up to you, and you find a place for it and tie it down.

"Is that everything?" you ask.

"That's all of it," your father says.

"Then we're ready to go. Where's Barnaby?"

"Here I am," says a figure emerging from the

shadows. It's Barnaby, and he's soaked to the skin and smells like a wine vat. He looks like a drowned rat.

"What happened to you?" your father asks.

"They didn't believe me," he says angrily. "They said dragons can't talk, then they dumped their wine on me."

"No one believed you?"

"Elmo and Modred, the bartender, believed me. They said they'd spread the word and meet us on the river road."

"I have half a mind to go after them, the drunken fools!" your father says, dabbing at your brother with the tail of his shirt.

"There's no time for that now," you say. "We need to leave. It'll be light soon, and we have to be well away from the village."

The wheels creak, and the horse strains as your wagon teeters down the rutted road. You meet a few of the other villagers by the river, and together you form a caravan as you head out onto the plateau, away from the village.

"Too bad more villagers didn't believe us," you say to Barnaby.

"Let 'em all stew in their own juices," your brother says sourly.

"Some people are just plain stubborn," your father adds.

But a profound regret steals over you. This isn't the way I thought it would be, you think. I wanted to save them all!

The town fades from sight behind you, full of friends you'll probably never see again and a house you'll never come home to.

Suppose we were going to ask the Storm Giant-ess for help, Finn," you begin. "How would we go about getting her attention?"

"Why, I'd just walk right up and rap on her leg, I would. Let me give you a hand. One has to be careful, so she doesn't crush you with her foot. We wee folk know something of these matters."

The giantess responds to your tap with a look of gleeful amazement.

"Well, I'll be switched!" she says, bending down to get a closer look at you. "Two more of the tiny creatures! And look at this one!" She reaches down to try to pick up Finn between her massive fingers.

"Excuse me, um, your ladyship," you say hastily, "but we have something very important to ask you. That's my brother you have up there, and we're on an urgent mission. We think you might be able to help us."

She bends down even closer, her huge green eyes fixed on you as you explain about the impor-tance of getting to the dragon Ayrie as soon as possible. When you've finished, she slaps her thigh and lets out an explosive laugh. "Hah! If that doesn't beat all!"

"We're serious about this, your ladyship. The lives of our friends and family are at stake. Is there any way you can help?"

Wiping a tear of merriment from her eye, the giantess says, "I don't know why you came to his lordship. Why, he wouldn't help a roc baby back to its nest, much less three little people trying to stop a dragon attack!"

"Apparently we were misled," you say, casting a glance at Finn.

"I'll say you were!" the giantess says. "Well, I don't know what I can do. I don't know much magic, and his lordship isn't home, so I can't convince him."

Suddenly you hear a commotion at the window, like the beating of wings. The giantess gets up from her chair and opens it.

In steps the largest, most colorful bird you've ever seen. It has the majestic look of a bird of prey, with talons big enough to encircle a cow, but it seems friendly enough. It hops up onto a perch nearby.

"Is this another of your pets?" you ask.

"More or less. This is Goff. He's a roc." She scratches the huge creature under its chin. "Aren't you, pretty birdy?" She pauses, stroking Goff's feathers thoughtfully. Then she smiles. "I have an idea. Do you feel like flying, little creature?" she asks you.

You look up at the roc. A bird that big could get you over the mountains in no time. "Do you think he'd take us to the Ayrie?" you ask.

"Goff? Sure. He'll do whatever I tell him, won't you, pretty boy?" she says, chucking the giant bird under his beak. "He's very well-trained."

"Would we have to ride in his claws?" you ask, nervously eyeing the sharp talons.

"I'll bet one of his lordship's socks would just fit around his neck. You could ride in that!"

The giantess leaves to find the sock while you and Finn climb the table to revive Barnaby. Barnaby is surprised to find himself in such odd surroundings, but remarkably enough, the idea of flying to the Ayrie aboard a roc seems to appeal to him.

"I've always wanted to fly!" he exclaims.

When the giantess returns and the sock is in place, Barnaby follows you into the sock, delighted with the idea of flying. But Finn seems reluctant.

"This is as far as I go, my friends. I promised I'd help get you to the Ayrie, and you'll soon be there, it seems. And once you get there, the way's pretty clear."

"Won't you please come, Finn?" you ask. "We may need you."

"Ah, you won't be needing me." He leans in close. "And besides I'm a wee bit afraid of flying myself. Gets me sicker than a dog. Good luck, you two!"

There's no more time to plead with him, or even to say goodbye. With you and Barnaby tied under its chin, the giant bird stalks back and forth, impatient to leave. With one breathtaking lunge, the roc is out the window. With one beat of its massive wings, the casement is only a small square of light in the darkness below.

Finn waves to you from the window. You

wave back, then you settle down next to Barnaby to enjoy the ride. In no time at all, you reach the entrance to the Ayrie.

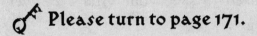 **Please turn to page 171.**

It's a hard decision whether you should let Finn try and work his spell. You've come to care about the little leprechaun, but in the end the need to save your village outweighs everything.

"It's a big sacrifice, Finn. Are you sure you want to go through with it?" you ask gently.

"Aye, that it is," Finn says, "a bigger price than I ever thought I'd have to pay. But I'm sure. You and your brother stand together, there where I can see you, and I'll try to remember the words."

Finn's eyes close, and he begins to mumble softly. Slowly the walls of the passageway begin to dissolve, and new walls take their place. You see torches burning in brackets high up in a large passageway, brackets that have been carved in the shape of the heads of dragons. You've reached the Ayrie at last!

You can no longer see Finn. His tiny figure has faded completely from view. He's a rabbit now, you think, or a woodchuck or a chipmunk. From now on, you'll look on forest animals differently. You'll always be wondering if one of them might be your leprechaun friend.

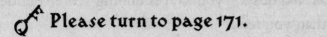 **Please turn to page 171.**

All right, Finn, we'll give it a go. Turn us into ghosts," you say, sounding more confident than you feel.

Finn's eyes roll back into his head, and his eyelids flutter, as he mumbles in a language you've never heard before.

A strange sensation comes over you. Your body begins to shiver, and you feel as light as a cloud—as if you could literally float away.

You look over at Barnaby to see that he's changed too. You can see right through him!

"Follow me, my friends," says Finn. He steps from the place where you've been hiding into the area where the ghosts are swirling like angry flags of light. They spot him and begin to sweep toward you.

"Begone, you filthy-souled spawn of darkness!" Finn cries out. "You can't be hindering me. I'm immortal! Go haunt some other poor soul!"

The ghosts hover close by, howling angrily, but none touch you as you follow Finn across the antechamber to the door of the Old Man of the Mountain's sanctuary. Finn knocks on the stout door with his walking stick.

The door falls open with a whine of rusty hinges. Behind it stands the Old Man of the Mountain himself, looking every inch the evil wizard, just as your father once described him.

"What do we have here?" he asks, knitting his brows menacingly over his baleful eyes. "A leprechaun?"

Finn closes his eyes once more and mutters something, and you and Barnaby turn solid again.

"Oho! Children too—from the village, no doubt," the Old Man says. "Well, I have no time for cheap parlor tricks."

He starts to close the door, but Finn quickly jabs his walking stick between the hinges.

"Not so fast, you old charlatan!" he says. "My friends here want a word with you. Tell him, Tory!"

In a trembling voice, you relate how you discovered the dragon and how it told the story about the impending attack on the village.

"And so you see, sir," you conclude, "peace has already been made between the dragons and the villagers. The dragons just haven't been told. If we can get to the Ayrie by dawn, we can convince them there's no need to attack. Can you help us? We need a spell to transport us there."

Your heart is hammering in your chest. The Old Man is every bit as terrifying as your Father made out. He stares down at you stone-faced, his eyes smoldering like hay fires. You wonder what he's going to do.

"I have friends among the dragons," he says. "Therefore I'm not certain which side I wish to be on in this matter."

"But there are no sides," Barnaby says. "There's no need for war at all."

"Silence!" the Old Man says, and Barnaby ducks behind you.

Finn slips inside the Old Man's inner sanctum and begins to inspect the books in the bookshelves. "Well, well, now," he mutters, pulling a book almost as large as he is from the bottommost shelf. "Are me old eyes deceiving me, or does this book belong to the Storm Giant?"

"Get away from there, imp!" shouts the Old Man, dashing toward the little leprechaun. Finn darts behind you for protection.

"Finn, you're not being very polite," you say.

"Nor will I be with the likes of him!" Finn says.

"I'd listen to your friend if I were you," says the Old Man, with undisguised malice in his voice. He draws himself up to his full height. "I'm going to retire to consider your request. Wait here."

He turns abruptly, crosses to a door in the far wall, opens it, and leaves the room.

"Thank goodness!" says Barnaby. "Now what do we do?"

"We wait and hope he comes back soon," you say. "Dawn can't be far off anymore."

"I wouldn't be worrying about dawn," says Finn, peering again at the oversized book. "With this spellbook, you'll be staring dragons in the face long before the dawn begins to light the sky."

"What are you talking about?" Barnaby asks.

"I know the language in this spellbook. I can do the spellcasting myself, but first we have to get out of here." He stuffs the book under his arm and starts for the door.

"Wait a minute, Finn," you say. "First of all, that book doesn't belong to us. Second, what about the Old Man?"

"That old windbag?" Finn says, and dismisses him with a wave of his hand.

"I'm with Finn," Barnaby announces. "Let's just take the book and go."

This is just great, you think. Should you trust Finn to use the book to get you to the Ayrie, or should you insist they wait for the old wizard to return?

If you want to wait for the wizard, turn to page 63.

If you choose to trust Finn, turn to page 91.

You glance back at Theron as he orders his friends to set up camp. He'd order Barnaby and me around just like that, you think. If he didn't want us to go, he'd stop us.

You decide not to give him the chance. Instead of telling him about the dragons and your urgent mission, you rejoin the hunters and remain silent.

The camp is quickly set up, and in a short time everyone settles down to eat. You've promised Barnaby he could have a meal, but now you don't know if you can wait for him to eat it. In your mind's eye, you keep seeing dragons swooping down and blasting the village with their fiery breath.

"We've got to get out of here," you tell Barnaby, "or we'll never make it to the Ayrie in time."

"Just a little longer?" Barnaby says. "I'm so hungry, and all I've gotten to eat is some bread and cheese. Let's stay for dinner. And maybe a nap."

"No," you say. "If we don't leave now, the village is doomed." Barnaby grumbles, but in a few minutes you've shouldered your packs, said good-bye to an astonished Theron, and are heading out of camp.

"You might at least have let me finish my meal," your brother grumbles.

The vast marsh is crisscrossed with trails and paths, and it isn't long before you find one headed in the direction you want to go. You follow it for about an hour. Coming out onto a low mound, you sit down to rest. Barnaby plops down beside you.

From the vantage point of the mound, you can see the entire marsh. It spreads out like an unbroken sea of grass all the way to the Aliwar Range.

"We should be off these flats and into the mountains by nightfall," you say. "The Old Man's retreat is just beyond those foothills."

"That means we'll get there when it's dark," says Barnaby, screwing up his face. "I don't like that idea."

"Me neither," you say, "but we haven't much choice."

You allow yourselves another ten minutes of rest before you begin to pull yourselves to your feet. If you're going to get to the Ayrie by dawn, you have to keep moving.

You reach for your pack, but instead of the worn leather strap, your hand comes to rest on something warm and moving.

You turn, startled. It's an arm, and it belongs to a little man, not more than two feet high, dressed in forest green. He's trying to steal your pack!

"Barnaby! Stop him!" you cry.

Even with your heavy pack in tow, the little fellow bounds off through the grass with remarkable speed.

Barnaby dashes after him, and you follow a short distance behind, trying to figure how to corral the little creature before he gets away.

"It's a leprechaun!" your brother shouts. "Keep your eyes on him! Don't lose him!"

The grass on the mound is shorter than the tall grass on the flat, but even so, the little man is small enough to disappear into it. You zigzag back and forth, trying desperately to keep him in sight. You've heard that, once spotted, a leprechaun can't use his power to become invisible as long as the one who spotted him keeps his or her eye on him.

The tiny man makes a turn in your direction, and you're able to get in front of him. He's so busy looking back at your brother that he doesn't see you until he runs right into your legs.

"Now I've got you!" you say, grabbing him by the arm.

"Good work!" Barnaby says, running up to join you. "But where's your pack? He doesn't have it!" He grabs the leprechaun's other arm. "All right, you little thief, where is it?"

"Easy, Barnaby," you say. "Let him talk."

"Aye!" the leprechaun says, putting a tiny hand to either side of his wee head. "Go easy there. I'm as mixed up as a fruitcake."

"Tell us where my pack is," you say.

"Valuable, is it?" the leprechaun says. "Full of treasure, perhaps? Or cakes?"

"As a matter of fact, it has a claw in it—a claw we took from a dragon we found dying earlier today."

"Hah!" laughs the leprechaun. "That's a good one, my friend! Some smelly carrion lover's dessert, is it? A piece of rotted flesh turning all green and moldy on its underside? Never prank a prankster, my friend. It'll do you no good."

"You don't believe me?"

"Not for one second."

"Then let me tell you how we came by that claw." As quickly as you can, you recount the events of the afternoon. When you reach the part about the attack on the village, the leprechaun's bushy little brows arch high with interest.

"So it's a mission of mercy, is it?" he cries. "Swordplay on the ramparts! Danger on the battlements! It's just what we leprechauns live for! Why, I'd give a pot of gold to be included in an adventure like that!"

"Nothing doing, leprechaun," you say. "All we want is to get my pack back."

But your brother interrupts. "Maybe it wouldn't be such a bad idea to have a leprechaun along. They're supposed to bring good luck, after all. We might need some luck tonight."

"It'll be dangerous," you say, turning to the leprechaun.

"I know!" the little man says jumping up and down in excitement. "That's the best part! Adventure!"

"There'll be no horseplay or foolishness," you say. "This journey is too important. You'll have to do as you're told."

"I will! I will!"

"All right, then. Where's my pack?"

"Why, right under your noses!" The leprechaun pulls back a veil of grass, and there lies the pack, nestled among the clumps of grass like a bird's egg. You pick it up and strap it on.

"All right, you can come. But I'm warning you, it's not going to be easy."

"Whee!" sings the little man, dancing so fast that his legs are a blur of motion. He grabs Barnaby by the arm, and they spin around together.

"It's a grand thing you're doing, my friends! A grand thing!" he shouts. "Finn's my name, and there'll be no worrying about me. Once a leprechaun gives his word, he's bound to it. And I give my word, I do, and freely. Now," he says, "where are we off to?"

"To see the Old Man of the Mountain."

"The Old Man of the Mountain?" Finn says. "Why, slay me! That evil wizard? What would you be wanting to see him for?"

"I've been wondering that too," says Barnaby.

"We need a spell to reach the Ayrie at Dragon's Eye Peak in time," you say. "Without some kind of magic, we'll never make it."

"Then it's the Storm Giant you'll be wanting," Finn says, "not the Old Man of the Mountain."

"The Storm Giant?" Barnaby asks. "Who's that?"

"From his mountain palace, he guides the storms as they pass over the mountains," Finn says. "It's an important job, it is. He's a friend of the dragons, but he's a fair-minded giant, he is."

You've never heard of the Storm Giant, but you know the Old Man of the Mountain, and you know the dangers of paying him a visit, especially at night. Should you change your plan now and seek out the Storm Giant instead? Or should you continue on to find the Old Man of the Mountain?

You're losing time and it's getting dark. You had better decide quickly.

⚷ If you want to continue on
to see the Old Man of the
Mountain, turn to page 108.

142

⚷ If you'd rather do as Finn
suggests and visit the Storm
Giant, turn to page 96.

There isn't enough time to go back, Barnaby. We'll have to cross the bridge. But let me go first. I'm heavier. If it can hold me, it can hold you."

Barnaby moves aside, and you step onto the first plank. The bridge groans under your weight.

The bridge is made of three parallel ropes: two that carry the planks, and a third rope that serves as a handhold and runs several feet above the others. You grab the handhold securely and take another step. Immediately you hear another loud creak.

You take two more steps, and the bridge sags perilously so that the handhold is now well over your head. You have to stretch to reach it.

Down below, the river churns like a boiling cauldron, flashing an eerie blue from time to time, almost as if it were magic.

"Careful there!" Finn calls, following your progress from the other side. "Hold on tight!"

"Don't fall! Hold on!" Barnaby shouts.

With a sound like a whip cracking, one of the ropes that supports the planks snaps in two.

Instantly the planks all point straight down. Several that weren't tied down plummet toward the river below.

You dangle from the hand rope, watching the planks fall. Your heart is pounding like a drum. If it weren't for the hand rope, you know you'd be falling with them.

"Don't move, Tory! I'm coming!" Barnaby cries.

"Don't!" you shout, glancing over and seeing him grab the hand rope. "It will never hold us both. I'm all right. I can make it."

It's a question of endurance now. The other side looks a long way off.

Hand over hand, you make your way carefully across the chasm, concentrating on the next handhold and no more. The rope is old and brittle. The fibers drive themselves into your fingers and palms like hundreds of little splinters, all urging you to let go.

"I mustn't look down," you tell yourself over and over. "I mustn't. If I look down, I'm sure to let go. I mustn't look down."

Finn is hunched over, watching anxiously

from the other side. You keep your eye on him and nothing else.

You think about your village and the dragons and the grave responsibility that by pure chance has fallen on your shoulders.

Hand over hand.

"You're making it! It's not far now!" Finn calls.

Hand over hand.

With your last bit of energy, you get a foot onto the ledge where Finn is standing and haul yourself up to safety.

"Well done!" Finn says patting you on the back. "Well done!"

Barnaby eyes the rope uncertainly, but he has no choice. He has to come across, and the rope is the only way.

Bravely he grabs on and swings out over the chasm. For an instant, he dangles limply, then he recovers and begins the same tedious hand-over-hand technique you used.

You hear a heavy thud behind you and turn around quickly. Finn looks up at you with startled eyes.

"Something is coming! Quick, behind this rock!"

At that very second, the hand rope supporting

Barnaby snaps. Out of the corner of your eye, you see him holding on for dear life as he swings rapidly toward the chasm wall.

You're paralyzed with indecision as Barnaby disappears from sight. Should you hide with Finn and hope that whoever or whatever is coming doesn't see the three of you until you can rescue Barnaby? Or should you throw caution to the wind and try and save your brother now?

If you think you should hide with Finn, turn to page 73.

If you decide to try to rescue Barnaby right away, turn to page 12.

As you try to decide, you take a long look at the fearful chimera guarding the door. Barnaby doesn't seem anxious to confront it, and you're not either.

"All right," you say. "Let's try to find Aurea." Carefully you make your way from pillar to pillar until you're safely past the chimera.

You continue down the corridor until you come to a room with a light on. You peer in and see a dragon sitting on a perch, high up near the ceiling. You're wondering if you should approach it, when it sees you and flies down.

"Humans!" it shouts. "Humans! Sound the alarm!"

"No, no!" you say hastily. "We're friends!"

But it's no use. In a matter of seconds, you're surrounded. More chimera guards lead you off to a dungeon several levels down. You try to get them to listen to you, but they push you roughly through a bronze door, then slam it behind you.

"Why didn't you show them the claw?" asks Barnaby.

"I tried!" you say. "I didn't get a chance."

"Claw?" asks a voice from the other side of the room. A dragon appears from the shadows. She looks somewhat haggard, but she has golden scales, just like Bosporus.

"Why, you're humans!" she declares. "The Ayrie's no place for you. We don't tolerate humans here!"

"We're not here by choice," says Barnaby grumpily.

"You said you had a claw. Where did you get it?" the dragon continues.

Quickly you relate the story of the dragons fighting in the valley, finishing by describing how Bosporus died and asked you to take his claw.

"Bosporus is dead?" the dragon says, obviously shaken. "This is terrible! And did you say he was coming back here to tell us that peace had already been made?"

"Yes. That was just before he was murdered by a dragon he called Clyto."

This last bit of information seems to hit the dragon particularly hard. She sits heavily by the dungeon wall and for several seconds stares blankly at the floor.

"I never would have believed Clyto was capable of such a thing," the dragon says. "His ambition is greater than I thought."

"Just who are you?" you ask, stepping closer.

"I'm called Aurea."

"Aurea!" Barnaby says. "You're the one Bosporus asked us to contact. He said you'd be able to help us."

"Obviously he was mistaken," says the dragon with a helpless shrug at her surroundings. "I'm trapped in this dungeon, just as you are."

The door bursts open and another dragon enters, followed by two chimera guards. You recognize him immediately. It's Clyto.

"So my sources were right!" he says. "There *are* human spies in the Ayrie."

"We're not spies!" shouts Barnaby. "We didn't even know dragons could talk until yesterday afternoon!"

Aurea is quickly on her feet, her tail slashing. "You'll never get away with this, Clyto! How long do you think it will be before the council finds out Bosporus has already made a pact with the humans' king?"

"How long? I would say never," Clyto replies. "In another few minutes, the council will have tired of waiting for Bosporus to return. Then they will vote to start the attack. Once we're in the air, the peace treaty won't matter."

"This is a dark day for dragons!" Aurea shakes her head.

"Guards, strip these spies of their weapons," orders Clyto. "I'll decide how to dispose of them later."

The chimeras take everything from you and Barnaby, including your packs.

"What do we do now?" asks Barnaby, once they're gone. "They've got the claw in your pack."

"I know," you say. "Even if we could get into the council meeting now, we'd have no way to convince them."

"It doesn't look good," says Aurea, then cocks her head, listening. "Interesting . . . I can hear the meeting through this ventilation shaft."

In a corner of the dungeon's ceiling, near Aurea,

you see a small round hole. As you approach it, you hear voices.

"Does this shaft lead into to the council chamber?" you ask.

"I think so," Aurea replies. "Why?"

"Because one of us might be able to climb up through it. We could break in on the meeting and tell the dragons the truth. Maybe we can stop the attack yet!"

Barnaby shakes his head. "We don't have the claw, remember? Clyto would just say we were lying."

"But we can't be any worse off than we are now," you say. "Any chance is better than none!"

"I think we should try to find a way to get Aurea out of here," says Barnaby. "They might believe her."

There isn't much time, you realize. From what you can hear, the council is preparing to vote right now. Even if you could get up the shaft, it might be too late. Should you try the shaft or try to free Aurea in the hope that somehow she can head off the attack?

If you want to climb the
shaft, turn to page 159.

152   If you decide to stay and
try to think of a way to free
Aurea, turn to page 180.

Ten feet down the left-hand shaft, you emerge from the narrow passage into a larger space. It's very dark, and it's difficult to tell how large it is. You're pretty certain you haven't been here before.

You start to climb back up, when the ladder, rotted with age, breaks beneath your weight, and for the next full second you're falling.

You land on something soft, something soft and sticky—a bed of some sort?—and for a moment you just lie there, thankful you didn't fall to your death or break a leg.

Relief quickly gives way to despair, however, when the hopelessness of your situation begins to sink in.

Now I've done it! you think. I go off on my own, waste valuable time, almost get eaten by a giant bird, and now I disappear into a forgotten mine shaft so far away from anything else that no one will ever find me. Meanwhile, the attack of the dragons goes on as planned! You could kick yourself for climbing up that shaft to begin with.

A movement in the darkness startles you.

Your muscles tense, and you hear a shuffling noise, like many feet moving at once. You strain to see what it could be.

You start to stand up, but whatever it is you've fallen into, it won't let you. It's sticky, like glue.

"No," you correct yourself, feeling the material with your fingers, "more like string soaked in syrup . . . or a . . ."

Your heart goes suddenly cold. "A spider's web!" you shout.

A terrifying equation appears in your mind. Giant egg . . . giant bird . . . giant web . . . .

An icy fear creeps over you. You thrash in the web, pulling at the strands. Finally you manage to get your feet onto solid ground. Then, as you stand up, you touch something hard in the web: a round ball, about the size of a dinner plate.

The giant spider, which you hear but haven't yet seen, begins to squeak noisily. Instinctively you draw back your hand. The squeaking immediately stops.

The spider's eggs! you think. No wonder it's disturbed!

You reach out with your hands and feel more of

the hard, round eggs. They're all stuck together.

I've fallen on a giant spider's egg sac! you think.

With the strength that comes from panic, you pull yourself free and begin to back away from the sac. The spider begins to shuffle, and from the direction of the sound, you can tell it's moved between you and its eggs.

"How do I get out of here?" you wonder.

The spider continues to move, scurrying to your left. To avoid it, you immediately sidestep to the right. Once again it moves, and again you sidestep out of its way.

Then your hand strikes something on the wall. A handhold! The dwarves must have used this room. The spider is herding you this way. It doesn't want you here any more than you want to be here.

Quickly you climb out of the spider's lair. Counting your lucky stars, you decide to go back and take the right-hand path.

Please turn to page 165.

F inn!" you shout. "Put away the book. We've decided to walk to the Ayrie."

"Walk?" asks the little man, staring up at you, eyes wide with astonishment. "You'll never make it. Not even at a dead run. Just look, my friends. It must be twenty leagues, maybe more."

"Oh, it can't be that far," Barnaby says.

"Oh, but it is, it is. This is most unfortunate. Why, a bit of magic, and I'd have you there safe and sound in a twinkling."

"Forget it, Finn. We've made up our minds," says Barnaby. He claps you on the back, and the two of you start off in the direction of the lights.

"Wait a minute!" says Finn, dashing along beside you. "Don't be afraid of magic. Why, where would we be without it? The sun comes up in the morning, the moon at night—what could be more magical than that? It's just that you're used to it, you see."

But you refuse to listen. Your mind is made up. Besides, the mountain already looks closer. You and Barnaby hike on, and after a while, little Finn follows at the rear, trudging along gloomily.

The book, which you went to such trouble to steal, lies forgotten among the rocks back on the flat.

You come to the edge of a high promontory.
Before you stretches a huge tract of land, clearly visible now but obscured earlier.

The mountain, with its lights on top, winks in the distance. From this vantage point, you can see how far away the Ayrie is. You realize you'll never be able to reach it by dawn on foot. Your heart sinks.

"Tory," says Barnaby softly, looking out over the vast landscape, "I really thought we could make it. I really did."

"I know you did. Never mind," you say, close to tears. You sit on a nearby boulder, your head in your hands. You wonder if Barnaby really understands what you've lost, the enormous responsibilities you've let slip through your fingers.

"Ah, my friend," says Finn, hopping onto a rock next to you and putting a hand on your shoulder. "Don't take it so hard. You gave it a try, you did, and a valiant one at that."

You look up, and through your tears, you see

the eastern sky is beginning to grow light, dabbed with splotches of bright pink.

Then you see something else that makes your heart almost stop. From the mountaintop in the distance, a line of black shapes is rising into the air. The first wave of dragons is on its way to the village.

THE END

The situation is desperate," you say. "I'm going to have to try the ventilation shaft."

Barnaby agrees, and with Aurea's help, you're soon shinnying up the inside of the shaft. When you get even with the council room, you realize that the chamber is deserted.

They must be up on the top of the mountain already, getting ready to begin the attack! you think. You're going to have to hurry if you want to stop them!

You continue on. As you get higher, you begin to hear voices.

"I promise you," the voice says, "brothers and sisters, the spies who killed Bosporus and tore off this claw shall pay the most severe penalty!"

It's Clyto! He's discovered the claw in your pack, but at least the attack hasn't started yet. There's still time.

You renew your efforts to climb faster. Up ahead, you see a small round hole covered with a grate. I hope it leads to the roof, you think.

"We will place Bosporus's claw here on the top of our ancestral home, in the very spot from which we are about to launch our attack to avenge his death!" Clyto's voice says.

You've made it. You can see the feet of dozens of dragons through the small opening. Bracing yourself, you push out the grate covering the hole and emerge in their midst.

"Wait!" you cry.

The dragons retreat several steps in surprise, all except Clyto.

"Here's one of the spies who killed poor Bosporus," he says, striding forward to confront you. "Obviously I didn't lock them up well enough."

"I'm not the one who killed Bosporus! You are! You killed him in cold blood so the council would never learn the truth: that Bosporus formed a pact of peace with King Olaf, and that the king has promised to move the village!"

"That's a lie!" Clyto shouts. "A bald-faced lie!"

"No, it isn't!" You look from face to face. It's obvious the other dragons don't believe you.

You wish you had the claw, but it's sitting on a rock beside Clyto, and the dragons assume you stole it. Even if you grabbed it and showed it to them, they still wouldn't believe you.

Then you notice something on Clyto's finger. It's the ring he took from Bosporus!

"Where did you get that ring, Clyto?" you ask. "Explain that if you can."

"It was given to me by a friend," says the dragon, trying to sound casual.

"That's a lie! That ring was given to Bosporus by King Olaf as a symbol of peace! You stole it when you killed Bosporus! I'll bet it's even inscribed."

"Don't be absurd," Clyto says, but several dragons nearby are eyeing his ring suspiciously.

"Which friend?" asks a thin brass dragon.

"You weren't wearing that yesterday," a silver-scaled female says, reaching for Clyto's claw. "May I see it?"

"Of course," Clyto says. He pulls the ring from his long talon and starts to hand it to her. Suddenly he drops it. It bounces once on the stones with a clang, and over the edge of the cliff. You rush after it. It's a thousand-foot drop. You'll never find the ring now!

"You did that on purpose!" you shout.

"I'm growing tired of your accusations," Clyto says, glaring at you. He draws a deep breath.

He's going to incinerate you, right here and now, with his fiery breath! You look around frantically for something to use to protect yourself. There's nothing around you but astonished dragons and the claw, sitting on the rock. You duck behind the rock.

The blast of Clyto's breath envelopes the rock, and only your hair and your shoes are singed. But on the rock, the claw turns white hot, and strange-colored smoke starts to pour off it.

"Why, it's just like it says in the legend!" the thin dragon exclaims as the crowd watches the claw burn.

"What legend?" you ask.

"It's said that burning the claw of a murdered dragon will call forth the victim's ghost, who will accuse his murderer," replies the dragon.

The smoke thickens, rises, and swirls, and in its coils, a figure begins to take shape. It's Bosporus!

He looks just as he did in real life, except for his missing claw. Meanwhile, the claw is taking on a transparent, ghostly appearance. Then, as the figure wavers, things begin to reverse themselves. The claw becomes more solid, while the figure of Bosporus begins to fade. Finally Bosporus is gone altogether, and only the claw remains. It twitches, tumbles out of the smoke, and lands at Clyto's feet.

The dragons all turn to face Clyto.

"Now, wait a minute," he says, backing up a step.

The dragons don't listen. They move slowly toward him.

You remain transfixed as you watch the dragons close in.

Suddenly Clyto takes to the air, soaring above the Ayrie. "Curse you!" he calls down. "Curse you all!" With one powerful beat of his wings, he's gone.

Later, when you go back inside the Ayrie to release Barnaby and Aurea, you fill them in on everything that's happened.

"And then he just flew off," you conclude. "The other dragons don't think he'll ever dare come back."

"I hope not," says Barnaby.

"Anyway," you say, "they believe our story about the peace agreement now. Our village is safe from dragons from now on, and the dragons can have their nesting grounds back!"

And, waving goodbye to your new dragon friends, you and Barnaby start the long hike down the mountain to your home.

You scurry down the right-hand shaft and are relieved to find Barnaby waiting for you.

"Tory, where have you been? You won't believe what we found!"

With the torch held high, he leads you down the tunnel. You hear a woman's voice singing in an eerie tone, like a musical saw. It sends a shiver down your spine.

"What is that?" you ask.

"Shh!" Barnaby leads you to where Finn and Oskar are hiding behind a fallen timber. Ahead, you see the strangest creature. A snake, with the head of a woman, is swaying back and forth, singing. Behind it is a strange bright light.

Oskar turns to you. "A naga," he whispers hoarsely. "We'll have to be careful. They're very poisonous."

"Aye—she's guarding a treasure, too, I'll warrant," says Finn.

"Is there some way around it?" you ask.

Oskar shakes his head. "The Ayrie lies beyond it. See that light? The treasure it's guarding is dragon treasure, for sure."

"We've got to figure out some way to get by it," says Barnaby.

Supporting itself on its coils and swaying back and forth, the naga reminds you of a worm trying to crawl out of the ground. That gives you an idea.

"I have a plan," you announce. "Go back to the shaft that leads upward, all of you, and wait for me there. I'll take care of this."

Your companions start to protest, but you insist. When they're gone, you take a deep breath and turn to face the naga.

Emerging from your hiding place, you approach the creature casually, then suddenly stoop and grab a handful of the gold it's guarding. The naga screeches as though its heart has been torn out. You take off at a run with the naga slithering after you.

You're amazed at how fast the creature can move. You have to run your fastest to stay ahead of it, down the long, dark corridor, toward the pinpoints of light that are the torches of your friends.

When you reach the shaft, you shoot up it and scramble for the surface. At first you're not sure that the naga saw you, but then you hear the scrape of its scales against the rock beneath you and its angry shrieks echoing in the shaft.

You climb like crazy, clawing at the ladder rungs, until you reach the fork you found earlier. You dart into the other passage and hide as the naga's long body slithers past.

Several seconds later you hear the naga cry out, but the cry is cut short as the screech of the giant bird echoes up and down the mountainside. Trembling with relief, you climb down and rejoin your friends.

"What happened to the naga?" asks Barnaby anxiously.

"An early bird got it," you say with a grin. "Now let's go back and have a look at that treasure!"

When you reach the treasure, Finn is already dancing on it, and Oskar is sitting on top of it.

"It's a ton and a half, maybe more, of pure gold!" shouts Oskar, picking up a handful of coins and letting them trickle through his fingers.

"We're rich! We're rich! We're rich!" Finn shouts.

"There's enough here to buy a whole new

village," the old dwarf says, "and then some!"

"He's right, Tory," Barnaby says, the gold twinkling in his eyes. "There's no need to go to the Ayrie now! We can return home, evacuate everyone, and replace whatever's lost."

"It sounds pretty easy," you say, "but first we have to get the gold home without being robbed, and then we have to figure out a way to distribute it fairly. It seems to me it might be better to go on to the Ayrie and prevent the attack in the first place."

"And take more risks?" Barnaby says.

You have to admit, Barnaby's plan sounds tempting. Should you give up now, take the gold, and go home, or should you continue on to the Ayrie?

If you want to take the gold and go home, turn to page 55.

If you decide to continue on to the Ayrie, turn to page 174.

You motion to your brother to back away from the bridge. "We can't take a chance on this rickety thing," you say. "We've got to go back to the Old Man's sanctuary."

"Good thinking," says Barnaby, looking more than a little relieved.

"What's going on?" calls Finn from the other side of the cavern.

"We're going back to the Old Man's sanctuary," you call. "Come on back."

Once more the little man hops on the rope of the handrail and prances across. "I don't want to second-guess you my friends, but I don't think this is a good decision," he says.

"But what choice do we have?" asks Barnaby. "We can't cross that bridge."

"You're just too big, that's the problem," says Finn. "I didn't want to say it before, but you're both unnaturally large."

"That's a matter of opinion," you say, laughing despite all that's gone wrong. "But we can't discuss it now. We've got to get back to the Old Man of the Mountain while there's still time."

An hour later, you're back where you started,

staring at the ghosts swirling before the door to the Old Man's retreat.

After all that effort, all you've managed to do is waste two hours. And when dawn comes, the dragons will mount their attack.

⚷ **Please turn to page 52.**

Now that you're inside the dragons' stronghold at last, you feel an odd combination of relief that a big part of the ordeal is over, but also dread because you know that now the real test begins.

You realize with surprise, however, that you don't know where to begin. You presumed that you'd just show Bosporus's claw to whomever you met, and you'd be taken to someone in charge. But it doesn't seem to be that easy. For one thing, the place is deserted.

"Where is everybody?" asks Barnaby as the two of you make your way up the long, silent hallway.

"I don't know," you reply. "It's sort of scary, isn't it?"

"You don't suppose they started the attack early, do you?" Barnaby asks.

You don't answer. You see a slight movement up ahead, and you motion to your brother to be quiet and to follow you behind one of the tall pillars that decorate the hall.

A creature is sitting in front of a set of ornately carved double doors, a creature you've heard about in legends but never thought you'd see in real life. It's a chimera, a monster with three heads—a lion's, a dragon's, and a goat's—all on one body!

Barnaby gasps. "I wouldn't have believed it if I didn't see it myself."

"Shh!" you say. "Listen to what the heads are saying!"

". . . until Bosporus gets back," says the lion's head.

"But they're not just going to wait in there all night, are they?" asks the goat's head. "Bosporus is already long overdue."

The dragon's head, meanwhile, has been listening at the door. "I think not," it says, turning back to join the others. "I think Clyto has just about convinced them to attack now."

"Did you hear that?" you whisper excitedly. "We've got to get in there!"

"Wait!" Barnaby says. "If we just rush in, they might believe us and they might not. Didn't Bosporus say something about a dragon named Aurea? Maybe we should try to find her first."

Maybe Barnaby's right, you think. You have no idea how the dragons will react to your story, and you only have one chance. If they don't believe you from the start, it may be very hard to convince them you're telling the truth.

On the other hand, you have no idea where Aurea is or how to find her. What should you do?

> ⚷ **If you want to try to enter the dragon council chamber, turn to page 100.**

> ⚷ **If you want to wait and try to find Aurea first, turn to page 147.**

I think we should go on to the Ayrie, however much treasure there is."

Barnaby starts to object, but you cut him off.

"Nothing's changed, Barnaby. We've still got to prevent a war from breaking out. If the dragons attack our village after the peace was reached, the king will attack the dragons. People will get hurt, even killed."

At first Barnaby says nothing. Then he nods his head grudgingly.

"Well, if you go to the Ayrie, you go without me," says Finn.

"What?" you say, surprised.

"You won't be needing me any longer. When you meet the dragons, it won't be luck or magic getting you through. It'll be justice, and justice is on your side."

"We can't go on without you, Finn," says Barnaby. You agree. The thought of not having the little fellow at your side is too much.

"Nonsense," Finn says. You'll face the dragons as bravely as you've faced everything else we've seen. I promised I'd get you to the Ayrie. The rest is up to you."

You try pleading with the little leprechaun, but it's no use. His mind is made up. In the end, you're forced to say goodbye to both him and Oskar. Then you shoulder your packs and start the journey to the Ayrie alone.

Soon you find yourselves in a spacious hallway, lit by torches flickering high on the wall. The torches are held in brackets carved in the shape of dragons, and you know you've reached the Ayrie at last.

Please turn to page 171.

You look down at Finn, lying motionless on the floor. His face is pale, and his lips quiver with exhaustion. Your heart goes out to him.

"We're just going to have to wait until he's recovered," you tell Barnaby. "We can't leave Finn behind. That's all there is to it. We're the reason he's in this condition."

"But what about the dragon attack at dawn?" Barnaby asks. "What about the village? Are we just going to forget about all that?"

"The lad has a point, he has," Finn says weakly. "Don't be hanging about here worrying over the likes of me. You two have a job to do."

"And we'll do it too," you say, "but first we're going to make sure you're all right."

From Barnaby's pack, you pull out a spare coat you brought in case it got cold in the mountains while you were scale hunting and spread it carefully over Finn. Then you and Barnaby settle down to wait.

Time passes slowly, and with each minute, your heart churns with worry and indecision. Barnaby feels it too.

"We've got to do something!" he says. "We

can't just sit here! Why can't we carry Finn in with us to see the Old Man of the Mountain? It's not as if he's heavy."

Finn overhears. "None of that. I can't see him like this. I'm a threat to him, I am, and right now I'm as weak as a kitten. There'd be no telling what devilment he'd cook up to torment me with. Nay, I'd rather die here at his door than face him without all my powers."

"What else can we do?" you ask, coming over and crouching beside the little leprechaun. "We could try to make it to the Ayrie on foot with you on our backs, except there's not enough time."

"We're just going to have to leave him, Tory. That's all there is to it!" Barnaby says. "We've got the lives of everyone in the village to think of!"

"No!" you reply sharply. "I'd rather carry him, even if we risk not making it in time. I just won't leave him, Barnaby."

"There's another way," says Finn, his voice weak. "I know a spell that will transport you two to the Ayrie, only it's a difficult one, it is. It'll take all I've got and then some."

"But will it work?" asks Barnaby.

"Aye, I think so."

"What about you, Finn?" you ask anxiously. "Is there any danger to you?"

"Oh, I'll go on, I will," Finn says. "We leprechauns are immortal, you know. Of course, I won't be a leprechaun any more—a rabbit or a squirrel, perhaps, or if I'm lucky, a big buck deer with antlers on my head as broad as tree limbs."

"But that's practically like dying!" you say. "No, I can't allow that!"

"But, Tory, look at him," Barnaby says. "He's not getting any stronger, and dawn isn't that far off. If we don't get to those dragons soon, the whole village will be destroyed! And Finn's willing to try the spell."

"Aye," Finn says. "When a leprechaun goes into a fight, he goes all the way, he does. I promised I'd help you get to the Ayrie, and get you there I shall, even if it takes every last bit of strength I have!"

What will you do? Will you allow Finn to sacrifice himself to get you to the Ayrie on time? Or will you carry him away from the Old Man's retreat and try to find some other way to get to the Ayrie?

If you want to let Finn work his spell, turn to page 128.

If you want to carry Finn and find another way to the Ayrie, turn to page 87.

A ll right," you say, "we'll stay, but we've got to figure out a way to let the council know Aurea is down here."

You begin pacing the room. "How many dragons know you're down here?" you ask Aurea.

"No one," she says. "I was taken from my room in the middle of the night. Clyto didn't want me at the meeting. He knew I'd never vote to attack."

You stop under the opening of the ventilation shaft. "If we can hear them, can they hear us?" you wonder aloud.

Aurea shrugs. "I'm not sure. This room isn't used very often. Contrary to what you might think, dragons don't throw each other in dungeons every day."

"What if we make a big ruckus?" you say. "If we made a lot of noise here under the ventilation shaft, they'd have to stop the meeting to find out what was going on, wouldn't they?"

"What good would that do?" asks Barnaby. "Clyto would only make up some story, then send some guards to gag us."

"But it's worth a try, isn't it? What have we got to lose?"

The three of you begin making as much noise as you can. You scream and shout and wail at the top of your lungs. The din in the stone-walled dungeon is deafening.

You're still screaming when the door flies open and Clyto stalks in. "What's the meaning of this?" he demands. "What do you think you're doing? Guards!"

Two chimeras enter the room. In their hands are three cloth gags.

"Are you afraid we'll tell them the truth about you, Clyto?" you shout as one of the chimeras grabs you. "That you're a murderer and you're starting this war for your own benefit?" You direct your shouts up the ventilation shaft.

"Shall we tell them how you killed Bosporus?" asks Barnaby, catching on to what you're doing.

"You think you can discredit me," Clyto says, smiling calmly. "I've already told the council about the human spies that were sent to stop us."

"Did you tell them about me as well?" Aurea asks, stepping forward. The guards rush her, but she backs away, her tail swishing across the stone floor nervously.

"Is this the way you begin your reign, Clyto?" Aurea presses on. "With murder and lies?"

"I'll be the most powerful ruler the dragons have ever known!" shouts Clyto.

"You'll be disgraced," Aurea says. "Your grave will be spit upon and scorned. You'll be forgotten."

"No!" Clyto shouts. He pushes the guards aside and lunges for Aurea.

At that moment, another dragon enters the room and sees what's happening. Shocked, he can only stop by the door and stare. Behind him, another dragon appears, then another. Soon, it looks like the entire council is here to see what's happening.

By this time, Clyto has overcome his adversary. He has Aurea pinned on the floor, her long neck under one of his powerful rear legs. Clyto rears up to attack Aurea when he suddenly becomes aware of his audience.

The room is filled with dragons now, and more are pressing inside every second. Clyto turns to them, a weak smile crossing his face.

"You'd better let Aurea go, brother," a large

dragon near the front says quietly.

Clyto steps back and allows Aurea to get up.

"Follow me, both of you," says the large dragon. "We'd better discuss this upstairs. Bring the human prisoners too."

Standing in the middle of the enormous council chamber, you explain to the dragons all you know about Bosporus, his death, and the agreement with King Olaf. When you've finished you're taken to a smaller room to wait with Barnaby.

It hasn't even been half an hour when Aurea comes to tell you that the attack has been called off, and that Clyto has been banished from Dragon's Eye Peak and will be forced to wander the northern wastes alone for the rest of his days.

"He'll be harmless enough there," says Aurea. "Meanwhile, give our regards to your village. Tell them that there will be no need to fear attacks from the dragons in the future."

"And you tell your council that we'll start moving the village off the nesting grounds as soon as we get back," you say.

"You two can be proud of what you've done for us," she says. "Your bravery and refusal to give up will live in dragon legend forever."

"We've learned a lot from you, too, Aurea," says Barnaby. "And we'll never forget you."

You say goodbye, then begin the long trek down the mountain, toward home, certain that there will be peace in your village for many years to come.

Don't argue! Please! There isn't time," you say. "Let's give Finn's instincts a try. We'll take the tunnel to the right."

"Very well," says the old dwarf, shrugging. "After all, it's your village that needs saving."

"He took that rather well, now, didn't he?" whispers Finn, turning to you with a sly smile. "All right, step this way," he says, skipping to the lead in front of Oskar.

The four of you have marched for only a few minutes before an awesome rumbling like thunder begins overhead. Rocks start to rain down on you from all sides. The old timbers supporting the roof give way, and for a moment it seems as though the whole mountain is coming down on your heads.

You huddle close to your friends, trying to shield yourself from the cave-in, when as abruptly as it began, it stops.

Finn quickly relights one of the torches with his magic while you and Barnaby beat the air with your arms trying to clear away the dust.

"Fine instincts you have there, leprechaun," Oskar says, coughing.

"Wouldn't be passing up an opportunity to say you told me so, now, would you?" Finn replies.

"Stop the bickering, you two!" you say. "Let's just be thankful that no one was hurt!"

"Say, look!" Barnaby says, pointing down the tunnel in the direction you were heading. The cave-in has knocked out part of the wall, revealing another passage, this one with a strange light glowing in it.

"Aha!" Finn shouts, hopping atop the rubble and peering through the opening. "What do you make of it now? Maybe my instincts aren't so daft after all!"

"Wait!" Oskar says. "There are creatures underground that you aboveground dwellers know nothing about. Some of them tempt their victims with lights just like that."

"Hogwash!" exclaims Finn. "Why, that's the way to the Ayrie. I'd bet my gold on it!"

"I'm not so sure," says the old dwarf, wrinkling his already deeply wrinkled brow. "I think we'd better go back to where we started and take the left-hand passage as I suggested. I don't trust those lights."

Another dispute is in the making here, and you can see you'll have to settle it. Should you retreat and take the left-hand passage Oskar urged you to follow earlier? Or should you trust Finn once again and follow the passage with the lights?

If you want to go back and take the left-hand passage, turn to page 21.

If you want to go toward the lights, turn to page 34.

I'm surprised you'd dare to take us before the council, Clyto," you say.

"You underestimate my hold on them," he says with a sly smile.

He calls a guard and has him tie your and your brother's hands and gag your mouths.

"This way," he says and nudges you with his long snout toward the council room.

The chamber resembles an arena with a stage in front, but instead of seats, perches are mounted on the walls. On each perch sits a dragon. In front of the stage, behind a stone firewall, burns a ceremonial fire.

This may not be as easy as Clyto expects, you think. When the guard tied your gag, you managed to keep some slack in it by pushing your jaw forward. It's getting loose. Just a little more wriggling and you'll be able to speak.

"Your attention please," calls Clyto as he marches the two of you onto the stage. "These spies were discovered outside our council room. Obviously they've been eavesdropping on us."

Indignant cries fill the room. Clyto motions for silence.

"This proves," he says, "that humans cannot be trusted. They must be destroyed!"

Angry shouts echo throughout the chamber. You glance over to see how Barnaby's taking all this. He stares wide-eyed at the audience as the angry dragons shake their claws at you. He looks terrified.

You notice not all the dragons are clamoring for war. Some sit on their perches, watching uneasily.

They must be for peace, you think. They're the ones you're going to have to appeal to.

You decide it's time to get rid of the gag. Clyto is too preoccupied to notice as you begin pushing it with your tongue. It doesn't take long before you manage to push it down out of the way.

"Members of the Dragon Council," you shout, "don't be misled! We humans are anxious for peace. In fact, an agreement has already been made between Bosporus and our king. Bosporus was on his way here to tell you about it yesterday when he was murdered by Clyto!"

The dragons are dumbfounded. They've stopped clamoring and are staring at you. Clyto's eyes narrow with hate. He starts across the stage when a voice calls out, "Let the human speak!"

"I myself saw Clyto do it," you go on. "Bosporus also told me, just before he died, that Clyto stole our king's ring from Bosporus's finger."

Hastily the red dragon covers his foreclaw. "It's a lie!" he shouts.

"I have more proof in the pack on my back!" you cry. Clyto looks horrified as a silver dragon, perched near the front of the stage, hops down and slices the bonds from your hands. You pull Bosporus's claw from your pack.

When the other dragons see it, they moan loudly, as if in one voice.

"Lies!" shouts Clyto, hopping onto a perch in the first row. "The humans killed Bosporus with one of their catapults! They killed him and cut off his claw!"

Confusion breaks out among the dragons. They don't know whom to believe. You hear loud, confused shouting throughout the chamber. In the midst of the pandemonium, you wriggle your hands out of your bonds and untie Barnaby.

The temper of the crowd seems to be turning against you. Clyto's supporters seem to outnumber the others, and the news of Bosporus's death has turned some of the holdouts to Clyto's side. Shouts of "Death to the murderers!" and "Attack the village now!" begin to reverberate on all sides. No one can hear you.

You remember Bosporus's final words: "If all else fails, burn the claw!" Quickly you fling the claw toward the fire.

Smoke explodes into the air and forms a column that rises up to the ceiling. A figure begins to take shape. You can hardly believe your eyes! It's Bosporus! He looks just as he did in life, except for his missing foreclaw, which he holds outstretched in his other front claws.

The dragons fall silent as the figure rises higher and higher in the council chamber. Clyto looks on, terrified.

As the figure of Bosporus reaches the ceiling, it begins to disappear, but the claw remains. Finally Bosporus's image disappears in the smoke, and only the claw is left.

It falls out of the air and lands at Clyto's feet.

The council gasps, and an uncomfortable stirring begins. The accusation is unmistakable. Bosporus has returned from the dead to name his murderer!

"No!" shouts Clyto, leaping onto the stage. Before anyone can stop him, he takes to the air. With one surge of his powerful wings, he's halfway to the hole in the roof of the chamber.

Not all of the dragons are dumbstruck however. A large gold dragon leaps from one of the highest perches and tackles Clyto. Clyto falters long enough for two more dragons to reach him and pull him back down to the ground.

"Let me go, you fools!" he roars. "You'll ruin everything!" Another dragon throws open the door and summons chimera guards to chain Clyto and haul him down to the dungeons.

The dragons are stunned, trying to digest all that's happened. For several minutes they're unable to do anything. Finally the gold dragon who's taken charge approaches you.

"Forgive us!" she says sincerely. "May we live in peace!" She reaches out her claw.

You take it, still numb from all that's happened.

"May we live in peace!" you say.

THE END